SOVEREIGN

THE WAYFINDER SERIES
BOOK 2

AMY ELIZABETH JOHNSON

Hard Cover ISBN 979-8-9986351-5-1, 979-8-9986351-7-5

Paperback ISBN 979-8-9986351-8-2

eBook ISBN 979-8-9986351-6-8, 979-8-9986351-9-9

 Formatted with Vellum

This book is dedicated to my Husband, Taj. I love you with all my heart. Thank you for being my adventure partner, soul mate, and best friend.

ALSO BY
AMY ELIZABETH JOHNSON

Blood of the Dragon

Sovereign

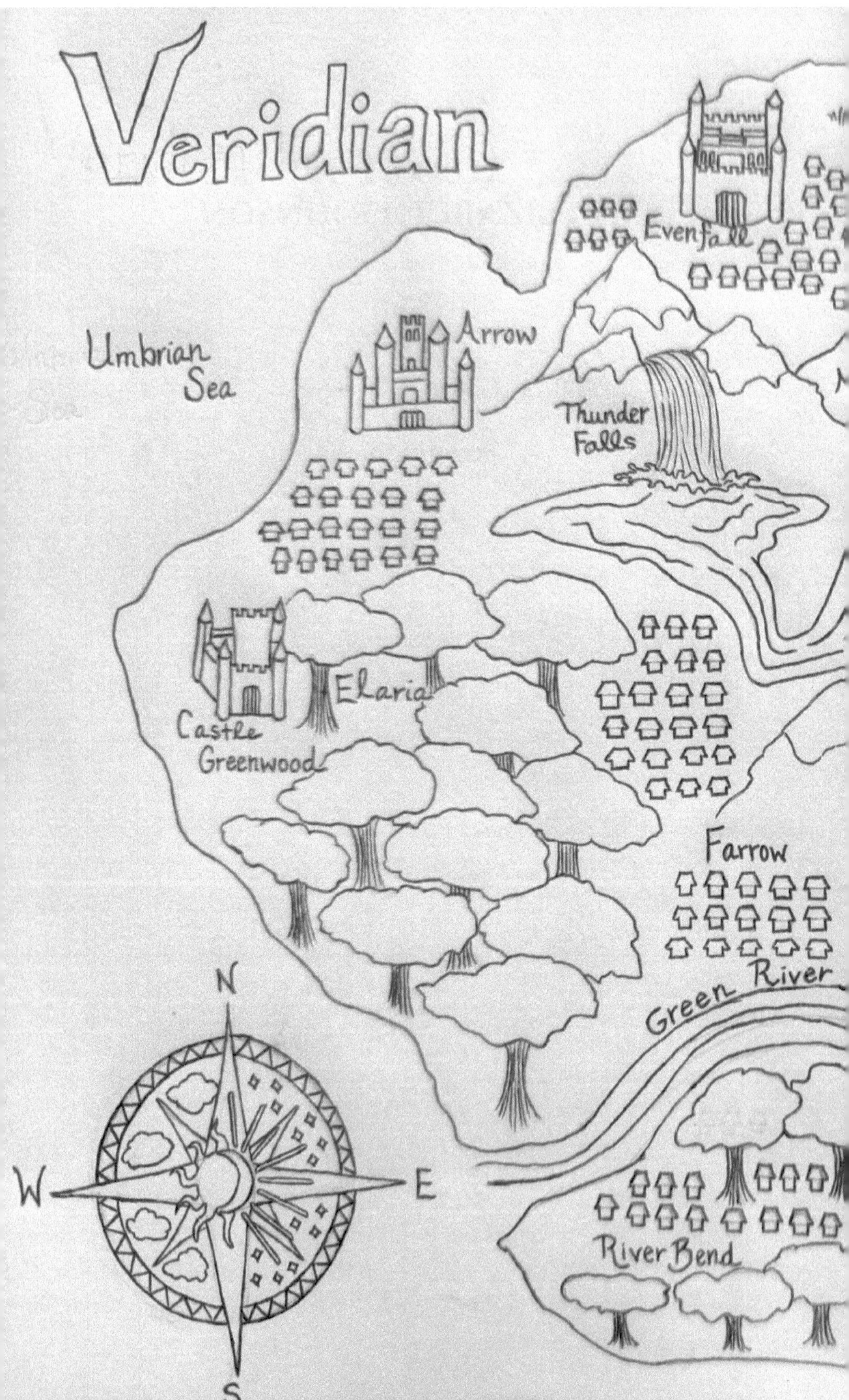
Veridian
Umbrian Sea
Arrow
Evenfall
Thunder Falls
Castle Greenwood
Elaria
Farrow
Green River
River Bend
N
W
E
S

Moorsend

Talon Lake

ilver Lake

untains

t's Tongue

Siren Sea

Red Mountains

Fang Forest

ge

tarling

The Black Keep

Caelen

AEW

1

IO

"You're holding back!" Terra taunts.

"We've been at this for hours!" I growl.

"You're free to go as soon as you land a strike."

I adjust my stance and give Terra a terse nod. Terra moves to her left, sword at the ready, light on her feet. I step quickly to my left, gripping my sword hilt tightly. I feel the anxiety gnawing at me. I watch her eyes. Terra keeps her eyes trained on mine as she lunges without warning. I hold my ground and block her first swipe. The clang of steel rings out across the meadow. The impact of her blow sends a shock wave up my aching arms.

I shove her back and swipe at her torso. Terra leaps back and flashes me an irritating grin. I charge, reigning blows down on her. My arms ignite with golden flames. Terra throws me off and vanishes into thin air. I listen hard. I see a small puff of dust to my right rise up. I spin and slash my sword into empty space. Terra reappears, examining a shallow slash in her leather vest.

"Aw, this one is my favorite," she sighs.

"Are you alright? Sorry, I'll replace it."

"I am fine. No need. Well done, Io. You are free to go."

"I just need a moment," I say sinking to the earth. I flop onto my back, my chest heaving.

My eyes slide shut. I feel the breeze on my skin. The wind carries the scent of salt and blooming wildflowers. I hear the grass rustle as Terra settles down beside me.

"We better get back before Rowan deploys a search party."

I snort. "Alright, let's go."

The sun is sinking into the sea. The waves churn and crash on the rocks below us. We reach the gardens, I pluck a red rose as we pass through. Felix slips us some warm flat-bread as we make our way through the kitchens. I nibble on my bread as we climb up to my tower chambers. Terra pushes the door open. My lips widen to a grin. Fast asleep on my couch is a softly snoring Rowan.

"I'll see you downstairs at supper," Terra says with a smile as she turns to leave.

I creep silently over to Rowan. I study his face, calm and peaceful. I lean down to kiss him and yelp in alarm as he pulls me down to the couch.

"Terra's had you on the cliffs for hours," Rowan scolds. "Let me assess the damage."

Rowan turns my hands over and inspects every inch of me for injury. I roll my eyes.

"She wouldn't let me go until I landed a

strike," I say with a shrug. "I assure you I am in perfect condition."

"For Terra's sake, I hope so," Rowan jests. "Lady Jen brought hot water for your bath. It should still be warm."

"Bless her," I say with a reverent exhale.

I remove my sword belt and start to strip. Rowan draws me into his arms. Our lips meet and I breathe in his familiar scent. Rowan runs his fingers through my wind tangled hair. I run my hands down his back. He pulls away and scoops me into his arms. I nuzzle his chest as he carries me over to the tub. Rowan lowers me slowly into the water. A sigh escapes me as I feel the delightful warmth spread through my battered body. *Maybe I'm not in perfect condition. My muscles are strained and several new bruises are blooming across my legs and torso.*

Rowan gently touches each bruise. I feel heat and then sweet relief from his healing magick. *My Healer.*

"Thank you," I breathe.

"Of course, my love. I can't have you limping to supper."

"I wasn't limping," I protest with a frown.

Rowan offers me a bar of soap, my favorite rosemary and peppermint. I wash myself and slip beneath the water to rinse. Rowan holds a towel out for me. I step out and wrap myself. I squeeze the excess water from my hair. I stand by the fire for a bit to dry my wet locks. I wander over to the wardrobe to select a gown for dinner. Lady Jen has added some new additions. I choose a silky violet gown with golden embroidery along the flowery bodice. I slip on my small clothes. Rowan secures the laces on my bodice.

We walk down the corridor, arm in arm. I have grown quite fond of the Black Keep. I have found several spots that are perfect for hiding when I want to disappear. My favorite is the hidden alcove in the library. I discovered it by accident when I was putting away some books. I touched a rather old leather volume with peeling gold lettering and a faded blue cover. The book slid back. I heard a soft metallic click, the shelves swung inward to reveal a little reading nook with a big window overlooking the sea. The window seat is piled high with squashy red pillows. There is a small writing desk with candles, parchment, and pots of ink with quills. I like to go there to read and nap.

Terra has taken up residence in her family's cottage near the sea cliffs. Her father and his accomplices disappeared after the attempt on the King's life. I train with Terra for several hours everyday. She has taught me the basics of swordsmanship, hand to hand combat, and archery. I am determined to be ready for Mara. She seems to have vanished without a trace. The soldiers we left behind to oversee the rebuilding of castle Greenwood returned months ago. The castle has been returned to House Greenwood. I see her in my dreams, dressed in forest green, holding a blade dripping in blood. I can smell smoke, the world is on fire. Mara smiles down at me. Her once kind eyes are full of rage and malice. She is not the girl I once called sister.

"Are you alright?"

I startle as Rowan brings me back to the present. "Yes, I am fine," I say with a nod. "Just thinking."

"I'm here if you need me."

I give his arm a gentle squeeze as we enter the great hall. Grandfather is seated at the high table. Mother is on his right, admonishing him about something. Selene, Rowan's mother, is seated next to my mother, suppressing a smile as she pretends not to listen to their squabble. Rowan and I sit on Grandfather's left.

"Ah, Io you're just in time to save me from your mother."

"What have you done now?" I ask with a smile.

"I have been on my best behavior," Grandfather huffs.

"Ha! You call insulting foreign dignitaries your best behavior?"

"Brigid, the man was unbearable."

"Just let me deal with foreign relations from now on, alright?"

"As you wish."

Servants sweep in with steaming platters of food. Mince meat pies, venison stew, fresh baked bread, roasted potatoes, butternut squash, and a large apple pie. A serving girl fills our goblets with honeyed mead. Rowan serves me some venison stew and bread before filling his own plate. I take a sip of mead and dunk my bread in some stew.

"Is there still no word on Mara?" I ask.

"Some villagers in Starling reported some strange happenings in the Glade, a clearing in the Cullen Woods where they hold their celebrations. Some hunters have gone missing. Vanished without a trace. Entrance to the woods is now forbidden. People who live at the edge of the woods have heard disturbing noises in the night. They believe the hunters were taken by a monster," Grandfather says.

"What does that have to do with Mara?"

"The villagers have spotted a woman in the woods. A young maid dressed in green, with green eyes, and auburn hair."

"What are we waiting for? We must investigate these claims."

"Rest assured Io, we have sent troops down to search the woods."

"I want to help."

"Absolutely not," Grandfather says firmly. "You are needed here. I will not risk your life."

"I can take care of myself."

"I do not doubt that, my love. I just want to keep you safe."

"As soon as I know more, you will be the first to know."

I let the matter drop. Rowan places a warm hand on mine. I lean my head against his shoulder. He kisses my forehead. I eat a few bites of stew. The sound of hurried footsteps catches my attention. Terra is walking swiftly to our table.

"Sorry I'm late," she says breathlessly as she takes a seat beside me.

I serve Terra some mince meat pie and venison stew. She smiles her thanks. Terra takes a long drink from her goblet.

"How is training going?" Grandfather asks.

"Io is making wonderful progress," Terra reports. "Her footwork has come a long way. She is lethal with a bow. She has bested me several times in hand to hand combat."

The way she barks at me in training I'd never know she thought so highly of me. I recall the way she whacked me with the flat surface of her blade when I forgot to protect my face while sparring. Rowan was furious. I told him that I was fine. Even though I could not lay on my back for a week. I did pin Terra a few times. Terra is a formidable opponent but, she has a tendency to get swept up in her emotions. A weakness I learned quickly to exploit. I have gotten quite good with my bow. I can hit every target Terra sets for me. I even practiced shooting from horseback. I prefer training to Princess lessons. My mother insists I attend them. I have given Mistress Bronwyn the slip several times, much to my mother's dismay. I have no interest in learning the sigils and words of the great houses. I have no intention of learning how to conduct myself as a royal.

2

ROWAN

The possible Mara sighting has Io on edge. I am sure she is planning on slipping out at night to ride for Starling. *My Firey Princess, no castle can hold her.* There is no sense in trying to talk her out of it. I pack quickly and dress. I am sure Terra will be waiting for us at the gate. I make my way to Io's chambers and knock.

Io opens the door. As I anticipated she is dressed, sword belt in hand and a pack slung over her shoulders. I raise a brow at her.

"What?"

"I knew you'd be off to Starling as soon as night fell."

"Are you coming or would you rather stand there and chastise my reckless behavior?"

"I'll chastise on the way."

Io smiles and steps quietly into the corridor. We head for the secret tunnel in the library. I pull on the sconce next to an ancient suit of armor beside the hearth, the stones scrape as they shift to reveal a narrow doorway and a winding staircase that descends into the underbelly of the Black Keep. I summon my blue flames to light our way, a brilliant blue fireball dances above my palm. The crackling of flames is a comfort in the dead silence of our earthen tunnel. Io lights her golden flames, holding her palm out proudly for me to admire.

"Terra has been helping me with my magick."

"It's beautiful," I say with a smile.

"Have you ever been to Starling?"

"Only in passing," I say. "One of the Kingsguard is from Starling, Sir Zane Harrow."

"Do you think it is really Mara?"

"Worth a look. What could she be up to in the woods?"

"I have a terrible feeling about this," Io says with a shiver.

"Whatever it is, we'll face it together," I say, taking her hand in mine.

Io nods and holds my hand tight. We emerge from the tunnel and step onto the deserted shore. We extinguish our flames. The waves sweep over the smooth stones, the pebbles and rocks rattle as the water slips back to the sea. The sky is lit by a half moon and endless twinkling stars. Io pulls her cloak around her. We head for the path that leads up the cliff face. A sheen of sweat covers my brow as we reach the top of the path.

"Would you two step lively? I nearly froze to death waiting for you," Terra says from her perch on a rock at the edge of the path.

"Ah, there you are," Io says with a laugh. "I knew you'd be along at some point."

"A grand entrance as always," I tease.

"Come on, I've brought the horses," Terra says springing to her feet.

Terra leads us to a small copse of trees where our faithful mounts await. King Eamon gave Io a roan for her 19th birthday. She named him Ash for his light gray coat and eyes. My mare, Nyx nuzzles Io's shoulder as she walks past. Io strokes her nose. Terra's mount, Ares stamps his hooves impatiently. *Always in a rush.*

We set off for Starling. Io closes her eyes and raises her face to the wind. We ride through the night by the light of the waxing moon. My senses are on high alert. It has been months since Io's encounter with Mara. *What are you plotting?*

The first streaks of daylight lighten the sky to a pale purple. Wispy tendrils of morning mist cling to the earth, our horses's hooves cut through the blanket of white, kicking up dark rich soil. I run my hand absently down Nyx's neck as we thunder through the woods.

"There! Up ahead!" Terra calls.

"Starling," I say.

"She's here," Io murmurs.

Io's eyes glass over, her breathing shallow. She suddenly goes limp and slips from her saddle. I launch off of Nyx and catch her before she strikes her head.

"IO!"

Io opens her eyes, blinking in confusion. Terra and I glance at each other with concern.

"Io? Are you alright?"

"I-I saw Mara," she says, squeezing her eyes shut.

I place my palms on her temples and send healing magick through her. I feel the tension in her body melt away.

"Thank you," she breathes.

"Where was Mara in your vision?"

"She was in the forest at Greenwood Castle," Io says slowly.

"Maybe she is planning her return to Elaria."

"We have to find her," Io says, trying to rise.

"Take it easy. You are unwell," I say, gently helping her to her feet.

Terra leads Ash over. Io pats his neck and swings up into the saddle. We walk the horses the last few yards to Starling. The village is waking as we arrive. A woman in a white apron collects brown eggs from a chicken coop. A little girl with corn silk colored hair hides behind her skirts as we pass. A man with a tanned face under a straw hat drives his horse and cart to market, it is filled with buckets of fresh flowers and baskets of pristine, red strawberries. Another wagon passes with a load of carrots and potatoes.

We follow the carts to the village square where the market vendors are setting up their stalls. I stop to ask a young man lighting a fire in his oven where we might find the village elder. He directs us to a hilltop on the far side of the village. A tall man with salt and pepper hair is stepping out the front door as we arrive. A slender woman with brown wavy hair and bright amber eyes stands on tip toes to give him a kiss. He holds her to his chest for a moment, whispering to her. The woman beams up at him, giving him one last kiss before they part. Io smiles at the loving exchange. The man spots us and walks forward.

"Good Morning. How may I help you?"

"Good Morning. I am Rowan McGlaughlin, Lord Commander of the Kingsguard. We've come at King Eamon's request. Can you tell me about these disappearances?"

"Aye, thank you for coming, good Sir and Ladies," the village elder says with a bow. "It's been nearly three weeks now since a group of young hunters disappeared. We found some of their things scattered about the Glade. There was no sign of struggle. We didn't know what to make of it."

"Have there been any other strange occurrences?"

"Several villagers have reported seeing a young maid walking through the forest. Pale complexion, green eyes, and auburn hair, dressed in a green gown and cloak."

"Has she spoken to anyone?"

"Not that I know of, Sir."

"Thank you, Mr.?"

"Anderson. Sean Anderson."

"We'll have a look around, Mr. Anderson."

We ride for the tree line behind the Anderson home. As we enter the forest, I feel my blood run cold. *Something is wrong.* I turn to speak to Io. She's *gone.* I look left to find Terra missing as well. *The Fae are playing tricks.*

I breathe deep. *Just keep moving.* I pat Nyx's neck to calm her. I push deeper into the forest, listening hard. A rustle to my right snatches my attention. I turn just in time to see a shimmer of golden light beneath an ash tree. I keep moving forward.

"Rowan!"

I kick Nyx into a canter, chasing Io's voice.

I pull her to a stop, she tosses her head in resentment over the rough jerk of the reins.

"It's not her," I murmur to Nyx. "It's a trap."

"ROWAN!"

I can hear the discrepancy now. It's not Io's voice. I have come to a crossroad. The false voice came from the left path. I steer Nyx down the right path. I hear rushing water. I catch glimpses of the river flowing swiftly through the trees. I decide to follow the river. Up ahead, I spy a piece of grey cloth snagged on a branch- a piece of Io's cloak. I cling to my hope that she is within reach. I search for any other sign of Io and Terra.

Suddenly something comes crashing through the trees on my left. I draw my sword and turn Nyx. A flash of blue and a tangle of blonde hair block my view as I am knocked clean off my horse. I land in the underbrush, I manage to hang onto my sword. I kick my attacker off of me and spring to my feet.

"Terra?"

"Rowan? Is it really you?" Terra asks as she brushes her hair out of her face.

"Of course it's me. What are you on about?"

"I was riding next to you and Io one minute and then I was lost in the mist. I heard Io calling me...I saw her in a clearing. When I approached her...she changed into a monster." Terra says trembling.

I walk over and pull her into my arms. I rub her back gently until she calms. I step away to look her over. The left sleeve of her shirt has been torn away, wrapped as a makeshift bandage around her bicep, blood trickles down to her forearm. There is a shallow cut above her right brow. I offer her a handkerchief to dab the blood. There is a bruise blooming under her left eye.

"What did the monster look like?"

"Like that," Terra says pointing over my shoulder, the color drains from her face.

I spin around and shield Terra. A massive creature on two legs, covered in black fur with long bloody claws and a wolf like face, steps out from behind a tree. A deep growl rumbles from his throat. Menacing yellow eyes watch us as he opens his jaws to reveal gleaming white teeth. He widens his stance and lets out a bone chilling howl. A high pitched whistle sounds in the distance, the werewolf winces and bolts off into the trees. Terra and I stand frozen for a moment.

"Well that was convenient..."

"Who called it off?" Terra wonders aloud.

"I'm not so sure we want to find out. We need to get to Io."

"There was no sign of her in this section of forest," Terra says, indicating the direction she came from.

"Let's follow the river. Maybe Io followed it to find a way out of the forest."

"Lead the way," Terra says.

Ares appears between some pine trees, tossing his head. Terra runs over and jumps in the saddle, affectionately stroking his neck. We ride along the river for several hours. The river seems as though it will never end. My anxiety grows with each passing minute. *Where are you, Io?* I hear a shout up ahead. Terra meets my eye and nods, we slow our horses to a walk. We dismount and secure our reins to the low hanging branches of an old oak tree. We creep closer on foot.

"We take her to the Princess!"

"What could she possibly want with this wench? Let's have our fun. She is no one. Traveling alone through the woods. Maidens disappear in the woods every day. She'll just be another tragic story."

"Our orders were clear."

"Fuck orders. And fuck the Princess!"

"So hard to find good help these days," a female voice drawls.

The two male voices fall silent. *The Princess, I presume.* Terra and I huddle beneath the brambles beside a pine tree. I can just make out two men dressed in green. The woman is on the far side of the clearing. I can see her swishing green skirts.

"Your Grace," one man falls to his knee.

The other man remains standing. The Princess chuckles at his act of defiance. She approaches slowly. We finally get a glimpse of her face. *Mara.* Terra squeezes my arm and I meet her anxious eyes.

"I do love a man with *fire,*" Mara says as she steps up to the man.

The henchman shifts uneasily beneath her unwavering cold gaze. Mara seizes a dagger from her belt and plunges it into the man's chest. His eyes widen in shock. Terra grips my arm but, does not utter a sound. I glance over at her, she does not look away. The man coughs, blood spurts from his lips. He sinks to his knees. Mara watches the light leave his eyes, knocking him backward with a swift kick. Mara closes her eyes and extends her right palm. Purple flames shoot from her outstretched hand, igniting the corpse.

Terra and I stare at each other with wide eyes. *Mara has magick? How is this possible?*

Mara turns to the kneeling man, "Harald, you've just been promoted. Bring the girl."

"Yes, Your Grace," Harald rises, he steps out of view.

Mara walks out of sight. Harald reappears carrying a limp figure dressed in a torn grey cloak. My heart clenches, *Io.* I move to rise but, Terra pulls me down. I glare at her and let out a disgruntled exhale.

"We'll follow them," Terra urges. "We do not know how big her force is, she could have an army on the other side of those trees."

As irate as I am, Terra is right. I relax and Terra exhales. We wait for the sounds of Mara and Harald to fade. When all is quiet we emerge from the under brush. Mara and Harald have vanished. We are right at the edge of the forest, the Green river snakes to the West. The Red Mountains are to the North. Caelen is behind us to the East.

Terra and I trace our steps back to where our horses are waiting. We untie their reins and mount up. We race back to the edge of the forest. *Where is Mara headed?*

3

IO

I wriggle my wrists, wincing as the rope chafes against my raw skin. Mara rides in front on a black stallion. Several guards ride between us. No one has spoken to me for two days. I have been desperately trying to transform to no avail. Something is wrong, I cannot access my power. There has been no sign of Rowan or Terra. I fear that something happened to them.

"Alright back here?" I startle as Mara pulls up alongside me.

“Doing well, thank you,” I say with a smile.

“Oh Io, I do hope you come to see things from my point of view. For old times sake. I would hate to have to kill you. It would leave a sour taste in my mouth,” Mara says with an air of boredom.

“What the fuck happened to you?” I ask not bothering to keep up with the charade of niceties. “What are you doing out here? Where is your family?”

“So many questions. You were always so eager. You might not like the answers,” Mara says.

“Try me.”

“My brush with death changed me. I no longer care to fit into the little life my parents carved out for me. It seems like you had a similar epiphany. We have always been opposite sides of the same coin.”

“I think our similarities died with you in the forest.”

"Tut, tut. No need to get personal. That is a bit of a sore spot for me."

"This all feels very personal. Threatening war and destruction. Your determination to wipe out an entire race because of our differences."

"Don't paint me as the Villain," Mara snaps. "Caelen attacked *us*. Destroyed OUR home. YOUR home! And you did nothing!"

"Elaria was where I lived but, it was never my home."

"You think they'll come to rescue you? Their *Princess?* You were raised by the enemy. You are a foreign invader. Once King Eamon falls, they'll cast you out like the traitor you are. You don't belong anywhere."

"And what of you? Where will you go?"

"I intend to take all of Veridian. I will unite the kingdoms under my rule."

"Best of luck with that. Don't expect anyone to kneel or worship the ground you walk on."

"They might not love me but, they will *fear* me."

Mara stares right through me. Her green eyes focused on a vision only she can see. She exhales heavily as her eyes come back into focus, she regards me with a cool stare. She seems possessed. A shiver runs down my spine. *This isn't Mara.*

"Chin up, Io. You have an opportunity to get back in my good graces. Swear fealty to me and I will see that you have a place in my new Kingdom."

"A generous offer," I scoff. "I'll lead the resistance."

"Even the proudest spirit can be broken. Don't waste your energy trying to summon your dragon fire. My Mistress taught me well. If you agree to play nice, I'll give it back," Mara says with a malevolent smile that seizes my heart.

I watch her ride back to the front of the column. *That vile bitch learned magick. Spectacular. I guess I'm on my own.* The heat of the day has everyone in a foul mood by noon. Mara orders a halt and the men scramble to set up a tent for her to rest. Mara dismounts and retires to her shady shelter. A beast of a man grabs me by the shoulders and pulls me from my horse. He drags me over to an elm tree and pushes me to the ground.

"Stay," he growls before stalking off.

The likelihood of success at an escape attempt looks grim. They took my sword, bow, and quiver of arrows. I close my eyes and imagine my scaly hide, leathery wings, and eyes of fire. I breathe deep, the sounds of the external world slip away. When I open my eyes, I am back on the sea cliffs in Caelen. Tears spring to my eyes. I breathe in the salt air.

"What's the plan?"

I whirl around to find the Goddess Hekate. She is dressed in a lovely navy gown with gold embellishments. Her dark hair is pinned up in an elaborate style.

"Any ideas? I could use a little help."

"You mortals are always so quick to ask for help."

"I have not given up," I protest. "I'll settle for guidance if you are reluctant to help."

Hekate laughs, "Magick cannot be destroyed. It lives in you. As long as you draw breath, your magick lives. No one can take your power, Io."

"How do I awaken it again?"

Hekate smiles, "You need only ask."

"That is rather cryptic and unhelpful," I say with a frown.

"Goddess guidance usually is," Hekate says with a small smile.

Hekate fades into a shower of shimmering stars. *I need only ask.* I clear my throat and close my eyes once more.

I know you're with me, please come to me now. I need you. I need to taste the fire.

I exhale and ball my fists in frustration. *COME ON! BE A DRAGON!* I can feel a small spark in my belly. *Burn bright. I am consumed by fire. Let the flames burn away my flesh and reveal my dragon form. Ignite.* The spark burns brighter. I feel the flickering warmth spreading from my belly to my chest, outward to my limbs. I open my eyes and whoop with excitement as I watch my skin harden into black obsidian scales. I realize with a start that I am sitting on the ground in front of the elm tree. I quickly scan my surroundings. Mara remains in her tent and the guards are playing cards by the cook fire. No one is paying me any mind.

I focus on my transformation. I feel like I am pushing against a heavy door, trying to force myself inside a fortress. I strain against an invisible force pushing me down, I feel my self sinking into the dirt. I dig my heels in and press upward. I picture my embers in my mind. I coax my fire into a blazing inferno. *Almost there.* A sheen of sweat covers my brow. Suddenly the ropes at my wrists start to smolder. Golden flames spring from my hands, burning my bonds to ash. I feel the pressure vanish. I slowly rise to my feet. The ground falls away as I rise to meet sky. I stand on four legs, my tail wraps around the elm tree, my wings spread wide. I can feel the fire in my veins.

The men are still absorbed in their card game. I slink over, towering over them. A slender man across the campfire looks up as I cast my shadow upon them. His mouth falls open, the pipe he was smoking tumbles to the ground. He frantically yanks his companion's arm.

"Luke, what the hell-?" The beast who helped me down from my horse, turns. We lock eyes.

Before he can open his mouth to scream, I wrap my spiked tail around his massive form and squeeze. My spikes pierce his flesh, showering his floundering companions with hot blood. They scream and scatter like frightened children. I uncoil my tail, flicking his bloody corpse aside. I crouch down and unleash a stream of fire. Their screams rouse Mara who bursts out of her tent in a nightgown. The incredulous look on her face is rather satisfying. I show her my teeth before I let out a deafening roar in her direction. Mara extends her right palm out, blue lightning dances across her finger tips. I light her up before she can unleash her power. The flames consume her, setting the grasslands ablaze. Thick black smoke rises into the air. I've lost sight of Mara. A clap of thunder sounds as a streak of bright blue lightning strikes the earth where Mara disappeared in the flames. Wicked laughter echoes all around me.

"IO!"

I raise my neck to look beyond the flames. Rowan and Terra are running toward the fire. Terra traces several complicated symbols in the air with her hands and thrusts her open palms toward the raging fire. A wave of water bursts forth, extinguishing the flames. I search the scorched earth for Mara's body. *She's gone. Of course she is gone. Nothing is ever that simple.*

I close my eyes and calm myself. I rein in

my fire. *Until next time.* I start to shrink back to the earth. The exertion of transforming crashes into me as I return to my human form. Rowan reaches for me. I fall into his arms, he holds me tight. The tears flow freely.

"Hi," I mumble against his chest.

"Hi," Rowan breathes, I can feel the smile in his voice.

"I was hoping I would not have to search too far," I say looking up to Rowan's face.

"We've been following you for two days."

"Mara's gone. She has magick." I report in a daze.

"We saw," Terra says wandering over to the smoldering grass where Mara was standing a moment ago. "This is advanced magick. How could she possibly wield it?"

"She said her Mistress taught her well. Not much to go on, I know."

"No," Terra admits. "But I've got an idea."

4

ROWAN

We find Ash among Mara's mounts. He is happy to see Io. I watch as she whispers to him. *I love her gentle heart.* She turns to me and smiles *that smile.* I would do anything to see that smile. I would level armies.

"Have I got something in my teeth?" Io asks with genuine concern.

I laugh. "No, you look lovely."

"Are you ok? You had a strange look on your face."

"I have never been better," I say grabbing her waist.

"The feeling is incredibly mutual," she says, her eyes gleam in the light of the setting sun.

I will always remember her this way. *Io Aurelia Flynn*, Daughter of Caelen, Bringer of Ash and Flame, The Blood of the Dragon. My *Soon to be Wife*. Gods willing we survive this world. *I will plant you a garden, where your flowers can bloom. Our children will have your wild spirit and fearless heart.*

Io swings up into her saddle. I follow suit. We join Terra on the path. I take the lead. We are a two days ride from Starling. Another day from the Black Keep. We'll ride hard into the night, a quick pace to cover as much ground during the cover of darkness. The heat of the afternoon burns out at dusk. A cool evening breeze soothes our horses. We stop to water them.

"I am fine to keep going," Io announces.

"Let's give the horses a break," I say.

"I'll get some wood for a fire," Terra offers.

Io loosens the back cinch on Ash's saddle. Ash neighs softly to convey his thanks. Io suddenly goes rigid, falling backward, the saddle lands heavily on her chest.

"Io?"

I rush forward and snatch the saddle, flinging it aside. Io's gone pale. A trickle of blood is running from her nose. Her skin is cold to the touch. Her breathing is labored. I press my palms to her chest.

"Stay with me."

Her breathing stabilizes as I channel my healing magick. The color returns to her cheeks. The breath rushes out of me when she opens her eyes. She looks around in a daze. Her eyes find mine and I see a flicker of recognition.

"Did I miss something?" Io asks softly.

"I'll catch you up later," I sigh, gently kissing her.

"You two can snog in the tent," Terra says, dropping an armful of firewood behind us.

"Apologies," I say with mock sincerity.

Terra rolls her eyes. She turns back to her pile of logs and kindling. Io sits up and dusts herself off. I glance at her with concern. I can see the pain in her eyes, the slight tremble in her hands. Her body is tense. She smiles at me bravely.

"You don't need to put on an act for me," I say firmly.

"I'm not as fragile as you fear," Io says with conviction.

"I can't lose you."

"You never will," Io says gazing into my eyes.

I pull her to my chest. "Not if I have anything to say about it."

I insist Io lay down. I am relieved when she concedes. She lets me carry her to our tent. I am alarmed when I see tears on her cheeks.

"Where does it hurt?"

"My heart," she whispers. "You've cracked it wide open."

"I can mend it," I say kissing her.

Io sighs against my lips. "Stay with me?"

"Always."

I lay beside her until her breathing slows to a deep rhythm. I kiss her forehead and step out of the tent. Terra is sitting by the fire. I take a seat opposite her.

"What was that about? Earlier."

"Io collapsed while she was removing Ash's saddle. I thought she was dying in my arms. Blood running from her nose, deathly pale, weak pulse."

"Poison. Or a spell," Terra says considering my words with a furrowed brow.

"Mara's magick?"

"Who is this Mistress she spoke of? We need to find out what we are up against."

"We'll regroup at the Black Keep. We need help. We can't do this alone."

"I have a few warriors in mind. Mages as well."

"I don't suppose you can talk Io into remaining at the Black Keep?"

"For the sake of your sanity, I would not get your hopes up. She'll be fine. She is strong."

"Of that I have no doubt. That does not mean I do not worry for her safety."

"She'll have us at her side. Go get some sleep. I'll take the first watch."

"Wake me when you're ready."

Terra waves me off. I find Io tossing in her sleep. When I touch her cheek, she is burning up. Golden flames dance along her arms. Io slowly opens her eyes, they are glowing like the smoldering coals of a fire. Black scales cover her arms.

"Io, wake up."

"Rowan?"

The flames vanish and Io's eyes shift back to her warm brown. Her scales fade back to warm brown skin. "What's wrong?" She asks.

"You have been unwell. Here. Have some water."

Io accepts the water, swallowing several gulps. "I feel fine."

"Rest. You need it."

"As do you. Come on. Get over here," Io says, patting the furs.

"As you wish, Your Grace."

"I insist, Lord Commander," Io says with an alluring smile.

I saunter over and kick off my boots. I sit on the edge of the bed. Io grabs my shoulders, pulling me down into a tangle of furs and limbs. I smile.

"I am relieved to see you are feeling better."

"I told you, I'm fine."

I lean in and kiss her. I taste her golden flames. We intertwine as the world fades away. There is only Io, my light in the darkness. When we have thoroughly exhausted ourselves we fall into a blissful sleep. What seems like several hours later a loud shout wakes me with a jolt. I launch out of bed. Io starts, looking around with wild eyes. I hold a finger to my lips. Io nods and slips out of bed.

I pull my boots on and grab my sword. Io

retrieves her bow and quiver. We slip out of the tent. I can see Terra on the other side of the camp fire, dagger in hand. She is speaking heatedly with a cloaked figure. Judging by stature and size the stranger is most likely male. I creep closer. Io moves to the left, staying hidden in the underbrush. She notches an arrow, giving me a nod. I move silently. Terra catches sight of me, her eyes flick to me and back to the stranger but, her face gives nothing away. The stranger turns his head, I do not give him the chance to move. I grab him from behind and place my blade at his throat. He holds his arms out to his sides.

"Easy, Rowan!" Terra cries. "He means no harm."

"And who do we have here?"

I release my captive, he slowly turns to face me. "Sir Xavier Fen, what business do you have in the middle of nowhere at this hour?"

"I am part of the search party that King

Eamon dispatched to search for the Princess. You wouldn't know anything about her whereabouts would you, Lord Commander?"

"Thank you, Sir Xavier," Io says emerging from her hiding place, returning her arrow to its quiver. "Please inform your party that I am unharmed."

"Yes, Your Grace," Xavier bows. "May I escort you home?"

"That would be wonderful. Thank you, we will break camp at once," Io says graciously.

"Rowan, will you give me a hand? Terra, why don't you and Xavier put out the fire?"

Terra glances at Io with a look of annoyance. Io smiles at her innocently. Terra grabs a bucket from our supplies and trudges to the gurgling stream down the bank. Xavier follows after Terra like a curious puppy. I shake my head as Io and I walk back to our tent.

"Playing match maker?" I ask without preamble.

"No," Io objects at once. She sighs, "I just

want her to be happy. She deserves that. Do you know him well? Is he a good man?"

"Xavier is harmless. Not an evil bone in his body. I don't think Terra is impressed by him though. She seems opposed to physical touch and companionship in general."

"Getting close to someone could be good for her," Io insists.

"Just let it happen naturally. Don't force it."

"I just gave her a little shove," Io shrugs. "It is up to her to make the connection."

"I wouldn't get your hopes up," I say.

"We'll see," Io says with a smile.

Io packs up our belongings and deposits them outside. We break down the tent, I bundle it up. Terra and Xavier return from the stream. Xavier pours water over the fire. Terra keeps her distance. She glances at him when she thinks no one is looking. I glimpse the ghost of a smile on her lips. I avert my eyes quickly so she does not catch me snooping. *Maybe there is something there.*

Io carries our packs over to the horses. She grabs her saddle. Terra joins Io by the horses. Xavier walks over to me.

"Need any help?"

"I'm good. How did you find us?" I ask.

"My gift," Xavier says simply.

He transforms into a massive grey wolf with glowing amber eyes. He rises onto his hind legs and shifts back to his human form.

"I tracked the Princess's scent."

"You are a good man to have around. Everything alright with you and Terra? It seems like you two may have met before."

"Only briefly," Xavier admits. "When we rode for Elaria last fall. She wandered right through our archery firing line."

"Ah, I see."

"She would not give me the time of day," Xavier says with a chuckle. "I was drawn to her though. Something about her, just stopped me in my tracks."

"I know the feeling," I say watching Io laughing with Terra.

"Well I hope you change her mind," I say.

"You and me both," Xavier says, gazing at Terra like a man thirsting for a drink of water.

Our new companion, Xavier is a pleasant addition to our group of misfits. He is hilarious. Io keeps her promise about not interfering. Her expression is one of physical pain as she watches Terra shoot down every chivalrous gesture that Xavier extends. I shake my head. It is painful to watch. I am tempted to intervene myself.

We meet up with the rest of the search party at daybreak. We pass through Starling and ride hard for Caelen. We send two riders ahead to reassure King Eamon that Io is safe and homebound. My mind wanders back to Mara as we press on. Teaching magick to a mortal is strictly forbidden. A crime punishable by death. Tensions between Elaria and Caelen date back to the dawn of time. Mortals who lust after magick usually meet untimely ends. Magick always comes with a price. A truth that most mortals uncover too late.

Magick is a gift. In Caelen it is believed that magick is bestowed upon a person as a mark of destiny. Magick was given to us by the Gods and Goddesses to help us.

The old legends say that in the beginning, all of Veridian was a land of magick. A wicked Queen grew jealous of her sister's power. She murdered her sister and consumed her power. The Gods punished the Queen. They stripped her of her magick and cast her into exile. Her name was struck from the histories. Over time, magick became rare. Less babies were born with the gift. Mortals without magick chose to step away from it. Elaria became a kingdom without magick. Boundaries were drawn. Magickal folk settled in Caelen. Through the ages wars and conflict have erupted. Peace was fragile. It has never lasted for more than a generation. Old wounds re-open. Rivalries run deep.

5

IO

When we dismount in the courtyard, my mother greets us with a tight lipped smile. "Welcome home."

"I'm sorry I worried you-"

"It's alright," she says tiredly. I feel a stab of guilt as I take in the bags under her eyes. "Your Grandfather is waiting for you in the council chambers."

"Understood." My Mother gives me a hug before departing.

"I love you," I say.

"I love you, little bird," she says touching my cheek with a gentle hand.

I watch her walk back to the steps. I try to imagine her as a child, running through the castle grounds. She seems so at ease here. *She left everything behind, for me. For a life with my father. What went wrong?*

"You ok?" Rowan asks.

"Just thinking," I say absently.

"I'll take Ash to the stables and meet you in the council chambers."

"Don't make me face him alone," I say, fighting a wave of anxiety.

"I'll be right behind you," Rowan reassures me. "Just walk slowly."

Rowan gives me a wink before heading to the stables. I exhale and head for the great hall. The council chambers are in the east wing, just past the castle library. I take my time getting there. Rowan appears out of a corridor hidden side door that somehow escaped my notice.

"How did you-"

"I'll show you. Right now we have somewhere to be," He says, guiding me down the corridor.

"And here I thought I knew the place."

"The Black Keep has magick of its own."

"You never cease to amaze me."

Rowan smiles that smile, the one that takes my breath away. He opens the door to the council chambers. Grandfather looks up as we enter. The other council members rise as we approach.

"Please forgive my intrusion," I say with a bow. "You requested my presence, Your Grace?"

"Yes, please join us," Grandfather says, indicating the empty chairs to his left.

Rowan and I take our seats. "What can you tell us of the rumors from Starling?"

"We found Princess Mara," Rowan says.

Relief washes over me. I squeeze his hand beneath the table to thank him for sparing me the burden of responding. All eyes flit between Rowan and Grandfather.

"We confronted her but, she escaped. The Princess has learned magick."

"Impossible," a red faced man exclaims from the far end of the table.

"I assure you Lord Sully, we witnessed this first hand," Rowan says firmly.

"What powers does she possess?" Grandfather presses Rowan.

"The Princess conjured fire and disappeared in a flash of blue lightning. She boasted that her 'Mistress taught her well.'

"This is an interesting development," Grandfather says gravely. "Io, what can you tell us about the Princess?"

"She is not the Mara I knew," I say flatly. "She is cold and full of rage. She is consumed by hatred. I have never seen her like this."

"Perhaps we can use that to our advantage," Rowan suggests. "Use her emotions against her. We can set a trap."

"What weakness can we extort?" Lord Sully asks.

"She lost her home. Revenge is poisoning

her mind. I think we need to discover this Mistress. It is possible that Mara is simply her puppet," I say.

"You are wise to think so, Io," Grandfather says. "There is more to this than we know. We need eyes on Mara. Lady Zaia, I have need of your unique skillset."

"How may I serve, Your Grace?" A tall red head, stands to address the King.

I examine her closely, she is dressed like a warrior, brown leather pants and low cut leather corset. She wears a long sword at her left hip and I spot several daggers on her person. I have seen her around the Black Keep. She keeps to herself. This is the first time I have ever heard her speak. I notice some of the men regarding her with wary eyes.

"Track Mara down. Infiltrate her ranks and report back."

"Yes, Your Grace," Lady Zaia bows deeply before taking her leave.

I watch her exit the chamber. I am still getting used to the level of freedom and respect that women enjoy here in Caelen. Back in Elaria women marry and bear children. Life paths are rather limited. Mara and I were lucky enough to experience life in Castle Greenwood. As handmaid to the Princess, I was educated and treated as a human being. Little girls in the villages were seen but, not heard. No better than livestock. Sold as brides or servants. Witnessing a woman carry out the King's bidding is extraordinary. It is pure magick.

Terra chooses this moment to enter the chamber and to my surprise, Sir Xavier follows. Rowan and I exchange a look. Terra tries desperately to hide her red cheeks. No one else at the table seems to think much of the two late comers.

"Apologies, Your Grace, Lords and Ladies," Terra says. She walks over to stand behind my chair. Sir Xavier stands beside her. Terra flashes him a look of exasperation as she takes a half step away from him. I suppress a smile.

"We will deploy troops to patrol the

boundaries of Caelen. Any transport or visitors seeking entry will be subject to search," Grandfather declares.

"It will be done, Your Grace," Lord Sully confirms. He rises from his seat and bows.

"I am sure we all have other matters to attend to," Grandfather continues. "Let us adjourn for the day."

The Lords and Ladies stand and bow to their King. I rise to go. Grandfather turns toward me. "I'd like a word, Io."

I swallow and wait for the reprimand. "Of course, Grandfather."

"You disobeyed me."

"I had to see for myself."

"You are a Princess of Caelen. You are a handmaid no more. You have many enemies, Io. You are not to leave the Black Keep without protection. I will not see innocent lives lost as a result of your reckless actions."

His brown eyes gleam, his stern tone makes me feel like an ignorant child. "Yes, Your Grace."

"I am glad you have returned safely," he says, softening. "You must be exhausted. Get some rest."

"I will. Thank you, Grandfather."

He smiles and I feel at ease once more. "You should do the same," I scold. "You look like some rest would do you good."

Terra and Xavier follow us out. "What kept you?" I ask casually.

"Someone had a little run in with a maid in the great hall," Terra says, shooting Xavier a dirty look. "Knocked a serving girl flat on her bottom and sent a whole tureen of chicken soup flying."

"It would have been rude not to help clean up," Xavier protested.

"You are trouble," Terra says, tossing her blonde hair over her shoulder. "You have a carrot in your hair."

Xavier plucks a mushy carrot from his curls as he watches Terra stalk off. "I think she likes me."

I laugh. "Don't give up on her."

"Wouldn't dream of it," Xavier says, never taking his eyes off Terra.

I study his face. He will be good for her. *Oh Freya, open her heart. He will care for it and shower her with love. She deserves to know what that feels like.* Xavier turns, retracing our steps.

"Where are you going?" I call after him.

"I've got an idea!" He shouts over his shoulder as he jogs out of sight.

"He is quite tenacious, I'll give him that," Rowan says.

"I'll work on Terra."

"I thought you were not going to meddle?"

"A conversation is not meddling."

Rowan kisses my forehead. "I love you. Let's lock ourselves away for a few hours."

"Lead the way," I say with a grin.

6

ROWAN

While Io rests, I walk down to the kitchens to find her some food. Felix smiles when I walk in.

"There he is, the man of the hour!"

"Man of the hour?" I ask with a raised brow. "You must have me confused with someone else."

"You're as good as Prince of Caelen," Felix insists. "Your Lady Love being the *Princess of Caelen.*"

"Titles mean nothing," I say with a wave of the hand.

"Title or no, I am happy for your boyo," Felix says offering me a steaming cup of mead.

"Thank you, my friend," I say, accepting the cup.

"To your Princess," Felix says raising a cup of his own.

"To my Princess," I say raising my cup.

We drink deeply. Felix loads a tray with plates of chicken and roast vegetables. "Here, being in love builds quite the appetite."

"It does indeed," I say with a smirk. "It's good to be home."

I grab some grapes and apples for us on my way out of the kitchen. I make my way back to Io's chambers. As I pass by a side corridor I catch a glimpse of two figures hiding in the shadows beneath an ancient tapestry depicting a map of Veridian. I stop and turn. *Terra and Xavier. Well done, it seems like his idea worked.* I walk on to allow them their privacy.

I quietly shut the door behind me, Io is

still fast asleep on the bed. I set down the tray of food. The fire is dying so I add another log. I slip off my boots and sink onto the sofa. I lean my head back and shut my eyes. A rustle of fabric alerts my senses, I tense as my eyes fly open.

"Asleep on the job?" Io asks playfully.

"You've caught me," I say snatching her by the waist.

Io giggles as I pull her into my arms. I gaze into her eyes. She opens her robe, the silk slides down her shoulders and puddles on the carpet. I drink her in, every luscious curve. I caress her bare back. She unbuttons my shirt. I remove my sword belt. Io unlaces my breeches. She straddles me, leaning in for a kiss. I press my lips to hers, losing myself in the taste of her.

"Marry me," I say, when we come up for air.

"After my crown?" Io jests.

"I'm being serious. Io Aurelia Flynn, I

came a live when I met you. That night that I found you on the hilltop, I thought I had found a fallen angel. You are like no one I have ever met before. You are kind, radiant, and fearless. A life without you is devoid of color. Will you do me the honor of becoming my wife?"

Io stares into my eyes, I feel as though she is searching the depths of my very soul. "Yes," she breathes. "Rowan Connor McGlaughlin I will be your wife."

I kiss her as I weave my fingers through her long black hair. I grab her hips and thrust inside her. Io gasps and wraps her arms around me.

"I love you," I whisper in her ear.

"I love you," she whispers, her lips brushing against my neck.

We end up on the rug in front of the hearth, a tangle of limbs. I trail my fingers down her back. Io sighs softly. We watch the flickering flames, reveling in the afterglow.

"Let's get married by the sea cliffs," Io says, looking up to me.

"As you wish," I say, closing my eyes.

Io trails kisses down my chest. When she reaches my groin, I crack my eyelids. "Ready for more?" I ask.

"Always," she says, taking me into her mouth.

A groan escapes my lips as Io explores with her tongue. She grips my hips as I ride the wave of pleasure radiating through me. Io meets my gaze, I flip her gently onto her back and hover over her heavenly body. She raises her hips and I ease into her. I kiss her breasts and caress her thighs. Io moans softly. She tips my chin up and our lips meet. The firelight reflects in her dark eyes. I move inside of her, pushing her higher and higher until she cries out in ecstasy.

"Good girl," I whisper as she clutches my forearms. "I'm not done with you yet."

"Take your time. You have me for eternity,"

Io breathes, her eyelids flutter closed, her rosy lips part slightly.

“I can do this for eternity.”

I lean down and kiss my blushing bride. *My Io, my Dragon Queen.*

We manage to peel ourselves out of bed and eat the food I brought up hours ago. Io takes a bite of chicken, she brings her hand to her mouth. The color suddenly drains from her face.

“Are you alright?” I ask.

Io jumps up and runs to the balcony. I rush after her. She vomits violently over the side. I hold her hair back for her. She sags against my chest once the the heaving stops. I help her back inside.

“Here drink some water,” I say offering her a cup from the table.

“Thank you,” she says weakly.

Io looks like she might faint. I take her face between my hands. The tension seeps from her as the healing magick spreads. I pull her in for a hug. When I pull away, tears are streaming down her face.

"What's wrong?" I ask in alarm. "I'll fetch the Healers."

"I'm late."

"Late for what?" I ask puzzled.

"My moon flow, is late," Io sobs. "I'm pregnant."

"Oh, Io. It's alright. That is wonderful," I say, smiling.

"Really? You're happy?" She says incredulously, swiping her tear stained face.

"Of course I am happy. Io, I love you. You will be an amazing mother. I am beyond happy to start a family with you," I say placing a hand on her belly.

She throws herself into my arms, knocking me flat on my back. "Hey take it easy, Mama." I say with a laugh.

"Don't fuss over me. I'm fine," she says with a scowl.

"Oh I will fuss," I say scooping her into my arms. "Does anyone else know?"

Io shakes her head. “Please don’t tell anyone.”

“I promise to keep our secret,” I say. “How far along are you?”

“Just a few weeks. Is there a Midwife in the Black Keep?”

“Lady Jocelyn, I’ll call on her. You just rest. Try to eat some fruit,” I say, offering some grapes.

Io manages to keep down her small handful of grapes. I help her into bed. I kiss her forehead. “I’ll be right back, love.”

“Hurry,” she says with a tired smile.

I walk briskly down the corridor. Lady Jocelyn lives with the Healers in the west wing. I am not sure how I can enlist her help without alerting my Mother to Io’s condition. When I enter the infirmary, Lady Jocelyn is examining a lady, heavy with child. I turn to allow the lady her privacy.

“My apologies, Lady Jocelyn, may I have a word when you are finished? I’ll wait outside.”

"Of course, Rowan. I'll be right out," Lady Jocelyn says in her kind, soothing tone.

A moment later, the pregnant woman emerges, I bow and she smiles as she passes. Lady Jocelyn appears in the door way.

"Come on in, Rowan."

I cross the threshold and take a seat at her work table. Lady Jocelyn closes the door and sits down, opposite me.

"How can I be of service?" She asks.

"Princess Io is with child, my child," I say. The very words set my heart racing. *I'm going to be a father. Io is carrying our child.* My lips spread into a dazed grin. *This is certainly a pleasant turn of events.*

"Oh, bless you both! What wonderful news," Lady Jocelyn exclaims, clapping her hand to her chest. "I am happy to help."

"Thank you, my Lady. The Princess would like to keep her pregnancy quiet for now. We would like to marry before we announce the good news. Will you examine her? She is feeling ill today."

"Of course, my son. Your secret is safe with me. I'll just get my bag," Lady Jocelyn rises from her seat.

We find Io sitting up in bed. She smiles when we enter. I am glad to see she looks better. Lady Jocelyn sets her bag down by the bed.

"Your Grace, I am Jocelyn Farrow, Midwife to the Black Keep," she says with a bow.

"I am pleased to meet you, Lady Jocelyn," Io says. "Thank you for coming."

"Of course, dear heart. Will you lie back for me? Yes, perfect."

I watch as Lady Jocelyn presses gently on Io's belly. I notice the slight swell of her lower abdomen. *Oh sweet babe. You are loved. You chose a truly extraordinary mother.* Io closes her eyes as Lady Jocelyn continues the exam.

"Everything is progressing nicely, Io. Plenty of rest. I know you are training with Terra. No need to stop living your life, just adjust as needed. Listen to your body. Rowan, make sure she is eating well. Treat her like the beautiful Goddess she is," Lady Jocelyn says with a wink. "Congratulations you two. I can't wait to meet your little one."

"Thank you, my Lady," I say with a bow. "I'll keep a close eye on her."

"Thank you, Lady Jocelyn," Io says. "I'll walk you back to the infirmary."

"I'll make my own way, sweetheart. You rest up. I'll check in on you in a few weeks time," Lady Jocelyn says with a warm smile.

Lady Jocelyn pats Io's shin as she stands. I walk her out. Lady Jocelyn gives my arm a gentle squeeze before she departs. Io is pulling on her riding pants when I enter the bedroom.

"Where are you off to?"

"Training with Terra," Io says firmly. "You heard, Lady Jocelyn said to live my life. I feel much better."

"I know there is no point in trying to stop you," I sigh. "Just promise me you'll take it easy and listen to your body as she advised."

"I promise," Io says, standing on tip toes to give me a kiss. "Walk with me?"

"Of course," I say taking her hand.

We head out to the sea cliffs. We reach Terra's cottage as the afternoon sun is starting to set. I knock on the door. Io and I exchange a look as we hear hushed voices within, one voice distinctly *male.* A few moments later Terra opens the door. Terra's hair is disheveled and her tunic is on backwards.

"Should we skip training today?" Io asks with a raised brow.

"Oh my gosh, I did not realize the time," Terra says, with a glance over her shoulder. "Yes, I'm just a bit distracted at the moment."

"Everything ok?" I ask.

"What? Of course, Everything is fine." Terra says with a wave of the hand. "I'll see you two at dinner," she says, closing the door in our faces.

Io and I retreat several paces before bursting out laughing.

"Oh my gosh, who can this mystery lover be?" Io gasps.

"I have a suspicion," I say slyly. "I saw Terra and Xavier talking in a side corridor in the castle. The moment seemed intimate."

"Oh you cheeky sneak," Io says elbowing me playfully.

"They make a good pair," I say with a shrug.

"They do," Io confirms. "Well it looks like I am following Lady Jocelyn's orders."

"Let's take a walk," I suggest. "If you are feeling up to it."

"Yes, I'd love to," Io says intertwining her arm with mine.

We leave Terra and Xavier to their love nest and head for the beach. The setting sun turns the sapphire waves to glittering gold. The clouds on the horizon are vibrant shades of orange and pink. Io glows in the sunlight, a radiant beauty. I caress her narrow waist.

"You are magnificent," I whisper against her neck.

"You are too kind," she whispers against my chest.

"I love you," I say, leaning in for a kiss.

Io sighs against my lips as I take in her intoxicating scent. Io presses her body against mine. I feel the fire spreading through my veins. Blue flames emanate from my hands as I explore her body. Io's golden flames flicker along her golden brown skin. Our flames join up and change to a sparkling emerald hue. *She always knows how to light my fire.*

7

TERRA

After King Eamon dismisses us, Rowan and Io retire to their chamber. I try to ditch Xavier but, he catches up to me with his ground eating strides.

"Hey, I'm sorry about making you late for the council meeting," Xavier says with annoying sincerity. *His kindness is off putting, I don't know how to talk to him.*

"It's fine," I say, not bothering to look over.

"Did I do something to offend you?"

"Not at all. I just like my space. Nothing personal."

"I'd like to get personal. If that is something you are interested in," Xavier says.

I stop to turn to him, "Look, Xavier. I'm no good at this sort of thing-"

"I'm not trying to make you uncomfortable. I just want to get to know you, that is all," Xavier says.

"I-I have never been with anyone other than Kellan. It was- complicated. You're better off looking for another woman. Trust me, you don't want to get to know me."

"I'll be the judge of that. Take all the time you need. I'm in no rush. You know where to find me."

I watch him walk down the corridor. I feel a stab of guilt and a glimmer of curiosity. My feet move of their own accord. He turns at the sound of my footsteps. I open my mouth to speak, a stab of pain in my head stops me short. I double over at the shock of intense pain in my skull. Xavier crouches down beside me.

"Terra!"

Xavier helps me to the ground and takes my hand in his. The pain plummets me into darkness.

"I've got you," Xavier says, his voice sounds far off. I can feel his gentle touch as he gives my hand a squeeze.

The darkness fades and I find myself standing in a burning field. A black dragon with smoldering eyes breathes a stream of fire over my head. Io. I drop to the smoking earth and cover my head with my hands. I feel the heat on my back as the flames pass over me. Io roars, her fury rattles my bones. I hear the beat of wings as she launches into the sky. A woman screams in the distance. I rise into a crouch. I see Mara running toward a tree line. She is badly injured. Io touches down, blocking Mara's path. Mara collapses to the ground. Io slashes at Mara with a curved claw. Mara shrieks. Io transforms back into human form. My mouth falls open as I take in her round belly. She is bleeding profusely from a wound in her left side. Io draws her sword and stands over Mara.

Mara raises her hands in surrender. I cannot hear her plea. Io crouches down. Mara passes a bundle to Io with shaking hands. I see tears streaming down Io's face as she gently closes Mara's eyes. She kisses Mara's forehead before she rises.

"Terra? Can you hear me?"

Black smoke blows across my vision. I cough as it fills my lungs, choking me. I wake with a start and stare up at Xavier's face etched with concern. He helps me into a sitting position.

"Hey, take it easy. Let's get you to the Healers."

"No. I just need a minute. It was only a vision," I say weakly.

My hands are trembling. I can taste the ash in my mouth. Xavier gently tips my chin up.

"You are not ok. Please let me walk you

home if you won't let me take you to the infirmary."

I nod in surrender. I try to rise but, my knees buckle. Xavier lifts me to my feet, gently holding me to his chest. I breathe in his scent of citrus and sage. It feels good to be held. *Maybe just a moment longer.*

Xavier pulls away to meet my eyes. My pulse quickens as I feel the heat of his body. I feel dizzy. He smiles a small smile. He steps away and I long for his touch. I resist the urge to close the distance between us. We walk silently through the castle. We reach the cottage all too soon.

Xavier opens the door. I step inside, he hesitates on the threshold.

"Would you like to come in?" I ask awkwardly.

"Do you want some company?"

"Sure, that would be nice," I admit, terrified at how vulnerable I feel in the moment.

Xavier keeps a respectful distance. He

takes a seat at the kitchen table. “I can make some tea,” he offers.

“Um sure, there is a kettle in the cabinet above the wash basin. I have some lemon ginger tea in the clay pot on the table.

“I’ll start a fire. Do you have any firewood?”

“There is a wood pile over there,” I say pointing.

I take a seat at the table and watch Xavier work. His forearms and biceps are strong. I feel my cheeks flush as my eyes roam over his broad back and round buttocks. I avert my eyes.

“How are you feeling?”

“Much better, thank you. I’m really ok if there is somewhere you need to be.”

“Nowhere to be. I am at you service, my Lady,” Xavier says glancing over his shoulder.

I smile despite my jittery nerves. I feel like a silly girl with a crush. *Get a hold of yourself, Terra. Bid him good evening and send him on his way.*

"Ah, there we go. That should do it," Xavier says turning away from the hearth.

"Thank you," I say.

Xavier smiles. He fills the kettle with water from a pitcher near the wash basin. He adds a scoop of tea and hangs it over the fire. He takes a seat opposite me at the table.

"I'm just going to lie down," I say. "You really don't need to stay."

"Alright. I'll wait for the tea and then see myself out."

"Thank you, Xavier."

"Of course. It's nothing," he says.

I walk to my bedroom and undress. I climb under the furs. I listen to the crackling fire for a while. I drift off at some point. The whistle of the tea pot rouses me. I hear the floor boards creak as Xavier retrieves the kettle. A moment later he carries a tea cup and saucer into my room. He sets the tea on the bedside table. I look up and our eyes meet. My heart is pounding in my chest as I slip out of the covers. Xavier exhales as he takes in my naked body.

“Terra-” he breathes.

“I’d like you to stay if you are interested.”

“I’d love to,” he says.

I pull him down to the bed. Xavier runs his hands down my back, stopping at my waist. I lift his shirt over his head and toss it aside. I run my hands over his chiseled chest and abdomen. Xavier’s draws in shaky breath. I slide my hands down to his groin. I give him a mischievous smile when I brush his hard cock beneath his breeches. I unlace his breeches, he slides them down as he kicks off his boots. We lay skin to skin as taking in every inch of each other.

“When I said I wanted to get to know you, I thought we might take a walk or share a meal.”

I laugh. “I would love to take a walk and share a meal. Should we stop?”

“I would like to continue if you are comfortable,” he says eagerly.

I stroke his cock. He groans, running his hand down to the apex of my thighs. He slides a finger inside me, I tremble in his arms. I guide him inside of me. Xavier is gentle. Every touch feels like a declaration of love. I feel like a Goddess being worshipped. I grab his hips as he thrusts into me. I arch my back, moaning softly. He claims my mouth, placing a hand on the side of my face. I pull away to gaze into his eyes. He gazes back with such intensity. I cannot breathe. I lose myself in those azure eyes.

"Terra, I really like you."

"I would hope so. Otherwise this would be rather awkward."

Xavier laughs and I join in. He brushes a strand of hair from my face. I lean in for a kiss. We warm each other up thoroughly. I rest my head on his chest when we are spent. Xavier trails his fingers down my back. I fall asleep to the sound of his beating heart.

A knock at the door jolts me from my peaceful slumber. Xavier's arms tighten around me. I look up to his sleep glazed eyes. I smile at him and he gives me a kiss.

"Should we just wait for them to give up and go away?"

"I'll get it," I say, searching for my clothes.

I pull on my pants and favorite tunic. I desperately try to blink the sleep from my eyes. I open the door to find Io and Rowan.

"Should we skip training today?" Io asks eyeing me with concern.

"Oh my gosh, I did not realize the time. Yes, I'm a bit distracted at the moment," I say glancing over my shoulder to look for Xavier.

"Everything ok?" Rowan asks in a fatherly tone.

"What? Of course, everything is fine. I'll see you two at dinner," I say closing the door before they can reply.

I hurry back to the bedroom where Xavier is sitting up in bed.

"I think you convinced them," He says with a smirk.

I jump back into the bed and pin him down. He stares up at me with those eyes as deep as the sea. I lean down and kiss him. We tangle up, beyond the need for spoken words.

8

IO

Rowan and I head back to the great hall for dinner. I usually enjoy meal times but, the smells emanating from the great hall turn my stomach. Rowan stops me short.

"Do you want me to take you up to bed? I can ask one of the kitchen staff to send some food up for later when you are feeling better."

"Yes, please," I manage to get out. I purse my lips together as I fight the wave of nausea that sweeps over me. I feel a light sheen of sweat on my forehead.

Rowan leads me to the staircase. Rowan opens the door to my chambers. I dash inside. I barely make it to the balcony before I vomit. Rowan helps me back inside. He places a bucket near the bed so I don't have to get up again.

"I'm sorry. Please go down and get something to eat. I'll be alright."

"I'll just get something from the kitchens for us."

Rowan kisses me before he leaves. I take a small sip of water from the goblet he left on the bedside table. I lean back on the pillows and close my eyes. When I open them the fire has burned down. I feel a nagging sense of dread. *Rowan should have been back by now.* I climb out of bed and rush down to the kitchens. Felix looks up as I enter.

"Good evening, Your Grace. Can I fix you something?"

"No, thank you, Felix. Have you seen Rowan?"

"Yes, he was here about an hour ago. I believe he was on his way to back to you. Is everything alright?"

"Yes, he must have run into someone in the corridor. I'll find him."

"Good night, Your Grace."

"Good night, Felix."

My anxiety mounts as I wonder where Rowan could have gone. I make my way to the great hall. Terra and Xavier are rising from a table. Terra sees me first.

"Hey, I was wondering where you were. You ok?"

"I can't find Rowan. I wasn't feeling well. He went down to the kitchens to get some food. He never came back."

"It's alright. We'll find him," Xavier says firmly.

We search the corridor leading to my chambers. We walk to Rowan's quarters and Xavier knocks on the door. It swings inward and my heart sinks. Xavier enters the room first. Terra takes my hand. A sob rises from my chest as I take in the room. It has been torn apart. The pillows and bed have been shredded, down feathers cover the floor. A trunk at the foot of the bed has been overturned. Terra pulls me in for a hug.

"Everything will be alright."

"We'll alert the castle guard. Terra take Io back to her chambers."

Xavier dashes out the door. I follow Terra back to my chamber. Terra helps me undress. One of the maids brought up some bathwater. I step into the tub.

"Rowan never keeps me waiting. Something is wrong."

"Don't worry-"

The door opens and Xavier appears in the doorway with a slumped Rowan leaning heavily on him. My heart stutters. Terra rushes over to help. I grab my robe and run over to the bed. Xavier lays Rowan onto the bed. His breathing is labored. He is slipping in and out of consciousness.

"Where did you find him?"

"Some guards patrolling the grounds

found him near the kitchens. They were taking him to the infirmary when I spotted them.

"Thank you," I say, my voice thick with emotion. "Did anyone see what happened?"

"The guards said they saw a cloaked figure dashing around the corner. They sent some guards in pursuit. I'll go see what I can find out."

"I'll help you with Rowan," Terra says. "Xavier will you send a Healer up?"

Xavier nods and rushes off. I ease Rowan's shirt off. I cannot find a wound on his torso. I check his head, my fingers come away bloody. Terra gently rolls him on his side so we can examine the wound. I dip a wash cloth in the hot bath water. I wipe away the blood and find a raised bump and shallow gash just above his right temple.

"Rowan? Can you hear me?"

"Io.."

"I'm here. I've got you."

"He'll be alright, love. It doesn't look life

threatening. I'll go to the kitchens to make a simple sleeping draft. A good night's sleep should help his healing powers speed up his recovery."

"Thank you," I say tiredly.

"I'll make some for you too."

"Don't let anyone in. I'll have guards patrol the corridor. Bolt the door until I return."

Terra leaves and I let out a shaky exhale.

"I'm alright."

I jump when Rowan squeezes my hand. "Are you trying to give me a heart attack?"

"Wouldn't dream of it."

"What happened?"

"I was leaving the kitchens and someone jumped me from behind. Black cloak, heavy black leather boots. That is all I saw before I passed out. When I came to the guards were helping me up."

I start to cry. Rowan pulls me down next to him, cradling me to his chest. "It's alright. I'm sorry I scared you," Rowan says, kissing the top of my head.

I calm myself and fall asleep clutching the front of his shirt. A knock on the door wakes me. I look up to see Rowan reclining against the pillows. Relief washes over me when I see he is alert and well.

"I told you everything would be alright," he says with a wink. He slips out of bed to get the door.

Terra enters holding two small glass bottles filled with a deep blue tincture. "Good to see you up and about. I brought a sleeping draft for you both."

"Thank you," Rowan says.

"Don't worry it is safe for pregnant women."

I turn to Rowan who shakes his head. "How did you know?"

"I didn't," Terra admits. "I had a vision."

"Please keep this between us."

"Of course. I'm happy for you," Terra says with a smile. She walks over and hugs me. "I guess this means we are planning a wedding?" She looks expectantly at Rowan.

"I actually proposed before I knew that I was going to be a father," Rowan says defensively.

"Good man," Terra says clapping him on the back. "I'll let you two get some sleep."

"Good night, love," I say.

"Get some rest, dear heart."

Rowan slips into the bath tub. I pick up the small vial that Terra left on the bedside table. I swirl the indigo liquid around. It looks like she collected drops from the night sky. I uncork it and take a small sip. It tastes like cherries. I lie back and close my eyes. I fall asleep immediately. The dreams come.

I am running through the forest at twilight. I can see a great bonfire up ahead. I hear drums, lutes strumming, the whine of violins, singing, laughing, and happy shouts. Women dressed in sheer, gauzy gowns that float around them like clouds. Men dressed in fine tunics and trousers twirling their beauties round and round. I smile at the sight. My eyes settle on a woman watching me from the other side of the bonfire. She is dressed in a lavender gown with a low cut neckline that accentuates her flawless figure. Her chestnut hair is unbound, falling in loose curls. Her green eyes glitter in the firelight. She turns and walks into the trees. I follow after her, drawn to her presence.

I lose sight of her. I weave through the dancers and step hesitantly into the woods beyond. There are candles everywhere, resting on freshly cut logs and stumps. Several lovers have retreated into the forest's shadowy embrace to continue their celebrations privately. I feel my cheeks grow hot as I do my best to tune out their sounds of passion. I settle down on a log. A small altar has been constructed at the base of a great oak tree. A loaf of bread, a cup of cream, and a jar of honey have been left among the burning candles. A small bundle of sage and several wildflowers have been arranged neatly.

"Such lovely gifts, left by those with so little to give."

I look up startled, it is the woman in the lavender gown. "Who are the gifts for?"

"For the Goddess Brigid, we honor her at Beltane."

"Beltane?"

"A celebration of fire and fertility. You have the gift of fire, Io. You have life growing inside you. We honor you as well."

"Who are you?"

"I am Runa, Guardian of Fang Forest."

"Well met, Runa. How do you know me?"

"Your family has lived on the edge of this forest for generations. House Flynn and the spirits of the forest have lived in harmony since the birth of Veridian. Castle Black was built with stones from the sea cliffs and wood from Fang Forest. It is imbued with the forest's Magick."

Runa produces a small leather pouch from her skirt pocket. "Take this. You will need it to defeat the Goddess Hel."

I take the small pouch from her hand. I loosen the draw strings and empty the contents into my palm. A strange emerald talisman carved with runes. "What am I supposed to do with it?"

When I look up Runa has vanished. "That is

rather irritating," I mutter to myself. I place the talisman back in the pouch and stash it in my own pocket. As I walk back toward the Beltane revelry, the forest begins to fade.

I open my eyes, Rowan is sitting on the edge of the bed. "Good morning, beautiful."

"Good morning," I mumble sleepily. When I sit up my hand bumps something under the covers. I push the blankets aside to reveal the small leather pouch that Runa gave me. I touch it to make sure that it is real. I loosen the drawstrings and empty the contents onto the bed. The emerald talisman glimmers up at me. The golden runes glow.

"Where did that come from?" Rowan asks examining the talisman.

"A woman gave it to me in my dream. How is this real?"

"Sounds like a question for Terra."

9

TERRA

I see the early morning light filtering through the gap in my curtains. The soft covers cradle me, I'll just linger a bit longer. A knock at the door ruins my plan. "Ugh," I groan as I toss the covers aside and drag myself to the entry. I unbolt the lock and open the door a crack. Xavier regards me with an apologetic expression.

"Apologies for the early hour. Rowan requested your presence. Says it is important," Xavier says with a shrug.

"I'll get dressed. You can have a seat in the kitchen."

Xavier heads for the kitchen while I trudge back to my bedroom. I splash some water on my face at the wash basin. I step into a simple blue gown. I pull on my stockings and boots. I grab a warm cloak as I drag a brush through my hair. Xavier rises when I enter the kitchen. His eyes seem to linger on me for a moment. He redirects his gaze. I tell myself I must have imagined it. We fight the gusts blowing in from the sea as we make our way to the gardens. Xavier walks near to my side, blocking the worst of the freezing winds. The kind gesture makes me smile. I take note of his hands remaining respectfully in his pockets. *I would not mind if he reached for my hand. I may even allow it.*

I sigh gratefully as we step into the warmth of the kitchens. Everything is still scrubbed clean from the night before, the pots and dishes are stowed away, the stone floors were swept and mopped with care. Felix is just starting the cook fires. Xavier hands me a honey wheat roll that he pilfered from a nearby basket.

"Thank you," I say with a small smile.

"My pleasure," Xavier replies with a smile of his own.

We walk through the empty corridors in a comfortable silence. Xavier knocks on the chamber door. Rowan lets us in. Io is seated by the fire, examining something in her hand.

"What is all the fuss about?" I ask dropping into the arm chair beside Io.

"Do you have any idea what this is?" Io asks, holding up an emerald talisman on a leather cord.

I feel a shiver down my spine as I see the golden runes shimmer. *It calls to me.* "Where did you get that?"

"A woman named Runa gave it to me in a dream. When I woke in my bed, I was holding the same leather pouch she gave me. This talisman was inside."

"I have seen these runes in an ancient

text before. This symbol represents *Yggdrasil, the World Tree.* I translate the other runes silently to myself. This talisman is said to ward off a great evil that threatens Yggdrasil."

"What are we supposed to do with it exactly?"

"I haven't the slightest idea."

"Any idea who would know?"

"Lita Magnuson. She is a very powerful mage and oracle. She has guided many a young mage. She lives up on Eagle Ridge."

"Great, let's go," Io says leaping to her feet.

"Hold on a moment. You are not going anywhere in your condition," Rowan says.

Io frowns, "My condition? I am in perfect health, thank you. You are daft if you think I will sit here while you get to have all the fun."

"Perhaps we should step outside?" Xavier mutters to me with a glance at Io's sparking eyes.

"Right behind you," I whisper as I start to rise.

"There is really no need for that," Io says with finality. "This discussion is over."

Rowan keeps his lips pressed into a thin line, his body radiating tension.

"Eagle Ridge is short ride from here," I say, taking pity on Rowan's frustration. "We'll bring an armed escort for additional protection."

"I can arrange for a carriage for Io," Xavier offers.

I give Io a pointed look when she opens her mouth to protest. "I think that would be lovely. Thank you, Xavier."

"We can leave tomorrow morning," Rowan says. "My apologies for disturbing you, Terra. Thank you both for coming."

"Of course," Xavier says, clapping Rowan on the back. "We'll see you two at the stables at first light."

"Take it easy," I say, giving Io's arm a gentle squeeze.

"Thank you," Io says, giving me a brave smile that does not reach her tired eyes.

Xavier and I move towards the door. I glance back to see Rowan taking Io into his arms. *Good man.* I smile as I leave them to pack. I feel Xavier's eyes on me. I look up to search his face.

"What?"

"I am just in awe of you," he says simply.

"No need for flattery, Sir. You've already stormed the castle," I say with an eye roll.

"I mean it," Xavier persists. "You have a way with people. You genuinely care for the people around you. It is one of the many things I love about you."

"You *love* things about me?"

"*Many* things."

"Such as?"

"Your eyes, I can always tell how you truly feel by the look in your eyes. The way you turn your face up to the sky right before you cast a spell. Your scent of sage and lavender. The way you flick your wrist before you draw your sword."

I forget to breathe for a moment as I listen

to Xavier. My eyes settle on his slightly parted lips. A smile tugs at the corner of his mouth as he leans in for the kill. When our lips meet, I shatter into a million pieces. My body trembles under his gentle touch.

"See," Xavier says breathlessly. "I can always tell what you are feeling when I look into your eyes."

"What am I feeling?"

"You love me, Terra Kade."

"You got me," I say, pulling him in for another kiss.

"I'll never let go," Xavier whispers against my lips.

I rise early the next morning to pack. I am just finishing up when Xavier knocks. When I answer the door, he pulls me in for a kiss. He kicks the door shut behind him. The world could have be ending outside and we would not bother to look out the window. His touch plunges me into the depths, I am utterly intoxicated by this man. I feel like an electric current is pulsing through me. My hands roam over his muscled back. I arch my hips up as he sends me over the edge. Xavier rolls onto his side. I curl up in his arms as our breaths intermingle.

"Hi," I say breathlessly.

"Hi," Xavier says with a laugh. "Ready to head to the stables?"

"Yes, let's make ourselves presentable," I say tossing his breeches at him.

10

ROWAN

I open my eyes to find Io already out of bed. *She probably feared I'd try to sneak off to Eagle Ridge without her.* I watch as she absently rubs the slight swell of her belly.

"You're beautiful," I say.

"Good morning," she says, walking over to the bed.

I sit up and pull her down to me. Io giggles as I kiss her neck. "You don't need to do this. I would feel better knowing you are safe from harm."

"And what makes you think I'll be any

safer in the Black Keep?" She challenges. "Where you go, I go. We'll keep each other safe."

"Always," I say, pulling her in for a deep kiss that causes us to linger in the warmth of our bed.

Once we are dressed and packed, we head down to the stables to meet our companions. Terra and Xavier are walking up as we arrive at the stables. I notice the way Xavier looks at Terra, the blush on Terra's cheeks as he whispers something that makes her smile. Io gives my hand a shake to draw my attention to the intimacy between them. I chuckle over her ardent enthusiasm. *That's Io, always wishing the best for everyone.*

As promised, Xavier has a carriage waiting. Io scowls at it. "I can ride just fine."

"I know you can," I say. "You just need to rest, for baby. I know you are still my fierce, fire breathing dragon princess."

"Don't forget it," she humphs as she climbs into the carriage.

I smile as she blows me a kiss from the window. I am relieved that she agreed. I watch as she settles in and closes her eyes. I knew she was feeling unwell this morning. I ask the driver to take the smoothest route possible. He promises to take extra care for the Princess. I pass him three gold coins to express my gratitude. He bows his head and gives my arm a firm clasp. I know what it is like to struggle. I know the coins will help keep his family fed. Maybe allow him to take a day of rest for himself.

I mount Nyx and give the signal to move out. We have ten knights with us. Four surround the carriage to protect the carriage driver and Io. The other six spread out to keep a careful eye on our surroundings as we ride. The sun is just breaking over the Red mountains when we pass through the West gate. We set a quick pace through the meadows, reaching the plains in no time. The Red Mountains are just beyond, the Fang Forest guarding their base. I can just make out the trail carved into the mountainside. Just above the white clouds conceal Eagle Ridge.

We take a short rest in the forest to water our horses. I peak in on Io, she is fast asleep. I find a cool cloth for her brow and empty the bucket I left for her. It looks as though the ride only worsened her morning sickness. I press a palm to her cheek and let my healing magick flow. The crease between her brows softens as she lets out a small sigh. The color returns to her face. I give her a kiss and cover her with a blanket. When everyone has broken their fast, we mount up and proceed to the mountain trail.

The air grows chill as we climb higher. The horses power up the steep incline, their hooves slipping on some loose rocks. Swirling clouds welcome us with open arms. The trail levels out at last, revealing a large stone house with a tall tower. I can hear rushing water nearby. Terra dismounts and leads her horse the rest of the way. There is a high rock wall and heavy wooden doors securing the perimeter. Terra rings a brass bell mounted on the side of the doors. The gates open to reveal a tall woman dressed in emerald green robes standing before a large fountain surrounded by red roses. Her lavender eyes light up at the sight of Terra, her painted lips curve into a warm smile.

"Hello, dear heart. Who have you brought to me?"

"Lady Lita, I bring Princess Io Flynn of Caelen. We have need of your wise counsel."

"Please come in and warm yourselves by the fire. I will put on some tea," Lady Lita says extending her arm toward a large purple door at the front of the stone house.

We all file in and take the horses to a barn a short distance from Lady Lita's home. The knights and I unsaddle the horses while Terra introduces Io to Lady Lita. Io smiles and exchanges pleasantries, I can see the great effort she is exerting to appear well. The men and I follow the women into the foray. Lady Lita's maids show us to our rooms.

"I will have hot water brought up for your baths," Lady Lita says. "Please refresh yourselves and rest. We will speak once you have settled in."

"Your gracious hospitality is deeply appreciated, my Lady," I say with a bow.

Lady Lita bows her head and leaves us. Io is exploring our chambers. They are surprisingly luxurious considering how far the castle is from civilization. Lady Lita wants for nothing up here. The feather bed is freshly made with soft linens and otter pelts. The canopy bed is surrounded by thick gauzy curtains. The ornate hearth is constructed from colorful river stones, a fire crackles merrily within. *It seems like she knew we were coming.*

Io walks over to the large window. "Come take a look at this view!"

Our room has a sweeping view of the Fang forest and the sprawling plains beyond. The morning sun has touched every inch of the land with his golden rays. The air hums with melodious birdsong. A wave of calm washes over me. I encircle Io's waist and turn her to face me. I place a gentle hand on her belly. She smiles up at me. I kiss my bride-to-be.

I insist Io lay down after she bathes. I know she is exhausted because she does not even put up a fight. She is asleep the moment her head rests on the pillow. I kiss her forehead as I draw the covers up. A knock on the door douses my hopes of lying with Io. At least I had not gotten undressed yet. I open the door and find Terra.

"Come with me. Is Io resting?"

"Yes. She just fell asleep."

"Let her rest. The sooner we meet with Lita, the sooner we can get back home safe."

I follow Terra down the corridor, we pass the staircase that led us to our rooms. We stop before a red door with roses carved into its surface. The craftsmanship is breathtaking. Terra pushes the door open. Lady Lita is seated at a large oak desk, several parchments are laid out before her. Every wall has floor to ceiling shelves stuffed with books, tinctures, and all manner of magickal oddities. A large pot is simmering away over the fire in the hearth. The air smells of cloves and allspice. Lady Lita rises to her feet to welcome us.

"Please come in, take a seat," she says gesturing to the leather arm chairs before her desk. Terra and I take our seats. Lady Lita sits, she waves her hand and a tea set appears. I am no stranger to magick but, the conjuring of morning tea out of thin air is impressive. Lady Lita fills three empty tea cups with an amber colored tea. A yellow plate is piled high with biscuits. Lady Lita takes a sip of her tea.

"Let us discuss the matter at hand."

Terra pulls the emerald talisman from her cloak, the golden runes pulse bright as Lady Lita takes it from her. She stands suddenly and walks straight to a bookshelf on the opposite side of the room. She returns with an old leather bound volume. There is a depiction of *Yggdrasil* on the cover. Lita lays the volume open on the desk, turning it to face us. The page has an illustration of the emerald talisman. My eye catches on an illustration of a woman casting fire.

"There is a legend about a great evil that will threaten the magick of this realm. Your enemy has no idea what she has set in motion. The true villain has yet to show her face. Our very way of life is under threat. If we do not stand against it, the world as we know it will cease to exist. This emerald talisman will give the bearer great power to defeat this evil. How did this come into your possession?"

"Io was given this talisman in a dream by a woman named Runa. When Io woke, the talisman was in her possession."

"It seems as though the Goddess Hekate has chosen our Savior. Io will need your help to succeed. And she will need your love, Rowan," Lita says looking at us with eyes of deep lavender.

"She will always have my love."

"I will see it done, my Lady," Terra says with a bow of her head.

"So mote it be. Rest now, my dears. You will need your strength."

Lady Lita hands the talisman back to Terra. I don't like this. Lady Lita is keeping something from us. Something that would change our minds about facing this great evil. Terra seems to be pondering the same thing by the look of her furrowed brow. We bid Lady Lita good night.

"She knows something that she does not want us to know."

"That is the way of Oracles. They are cursed with the sight. They see terrible fates. No good ever comes from revealing more than what is necessary."

"So they send people to their deaths unknowingly?" I ask, my tone a little sharper than I intend.

Terra places a gentle hand on my forearm. "I won't let any harm come to Io. I swear it to you, Rowan. I will keep her safe at all costs."

I stare into Terra's intense, icy blue gaze. My rising emotions rob me of speech so I simply nod. Terra and I part ways in the corridor. I return to Io, fast asleep where I left her. I undress and quickly bathe. I climb into bed beside her. I kiss her forehead. Io murmurs in her sleep, nuzzling closer to me. *We will face whatever comes, together. We have our whole lives to live. Nothing will keep us apart.* I close my eyes, sleep takes me.

11

IO

I wake up in Rowan's arms, his face relaxed in deep sleep. Night has fallen. I slide out of bed, careful not to disturb my husband-to-be. I lean down and kiss him on the forehead. I rifle through my pack for some clothes. I settle for some comfortable dark green pants and a white cotton shirt. I fasten my cloak and grab my boots. I close the chamber door softly. I pull on my socks and boots. Relieved to have some energy at last, I cannot possibly sit still. I wander through the corridors. The spacious interior of the castle does not seem possible by the impression given by the structure's outward appearance. *An enchanted castle.*

"Can't sleep?"

I jump and spin around to stare at a woman in emerald green robes with striking lavender eyes. "Hello Lady Lita."

"I apologize for the fright."

"I am fine. Forgive me for my wanderings. I just needed some air."

"Of course. Would you like to step out into the gardens?"

"That would be lovely, thank you."

Lady Lita leads me through an enormous stone archway into the most exquisite garden I have ever laid eyes on. Fairies flit from flower to flower. Fireflies twinkle among pristine pink tulips. Herbs give off a lovely aroma. Wildflowers spill from their beds. A fountain with a statue of the Goddess Hekate draws my eye. Lady Lita leads me to a wooden bench swing. We take a seat like old friends.

"Your garden is divine."

"It is my favorite place," Lady Lita says with a serene smile.

"What troubles you, my dear?"

"I am afraid that all the blessings I have received of late will be taken from me."

"Do not live in fear, child. Trust in the Divine Plan. Everything you need, you already possess. Face everything and rise."

I smile at Lita's words. They do not extinguish my worries but, they kindle a spark of hope.

"You have a great destiny, Io. The path is laid before you. You only need take the first step. The way will be revealed to you."

"I want no part of this great destiny. I want to live in peace with my family."

"Peace is often hard won by those who have the power to change the world for the better."

Lady Lita regards me with a compassionate smile. "Here take this. It will help with your morning sickness. There is hope.

Do not lose faith. You were born to do this."

"Thank you," I murmur as Lita places a small glass bottle in my hand.

Lady Lita rises and offers me her hand. I place my hand in hers and she gasps, her eyes glaze over. She squeezes my hand tightly.

"Lita? What is it?" I try to withdraw my hand but, her grip tightens painfully. "Lita!"

Lita blinks and releases my hand. I grab her by the shoulders to steady her. "You must return to Caelen. Now! She is coming."

I run back to my chamber. Lita rushes off to wake the stable boys to ready our horses. I burst into the bedchamber. Rowan sits bolt upright in bed brandishing a dagger. He looks me over, visibly relaxing when he sees that I am unharmed.

"Io, what's wrong?"

"Lady Lita, had a vision. She says we must return to Caelen at once. Mara is heading for the Black Keep!"

We stuff our belongings into our packs and dash out the door. Terra and Xavier meet us in the corridor. I make no comment on the fact that Xavier emerged from Terra's bed chamber. We get down to the stables where our men are ready. The knights mount up. The carriage driver has readied the carriage. I roll my eyes at the sight of it.

"Ride ahead and render aid. I'll catch up," I say to my companions.

I climb into the carriage and watch the others ride off. The driver follows after at an infuriatingly slow pace. I bide my time to make sure the others are far ahead.

"Driver! Stop the carriage, please."

The carriage slows and I hop out. "Princess, is there a problem?"

"No problem, at all good Sir. Merely a change of plan. Please take this as a token of my gratitude for your fine services," I say tossing him a pouch of coins. "Take care on the road!"

Before he can reply I take off running, the tall grass brushes against my pants legs. I close my eyes and reach for my fire. Skin turns to scales as my body shifts from human to dragon. I spread my wings and launch into the night sky. I spy the stunned driver and four mounted knights gawking up at me as I set a course back to Caelen. I climb high above the clouds to escape the notice of my companions on horseback. The chill night air does not bother me in the slightest. A stream of steam escapes my nostrils as I fly onward. It is not long before Caelen appears on the horizon. My heart seizes as I take in the horrific scene below, Caelen is *burning.* The villages are ablaze. Enemy troops are storming the Black Keep. I dive down.

There is no sign of my companions but, I cannot wait. I continue on to defend the keep. I land in the courtyard and unleash a thunderous roar. Several enemy soldiers rush me, armed with swords, bows, and spears. I greet them with a stream of fire.

Screams fill the air as the flames feast on their flesh. I swipe my tail and knock a line of men into the keep's perimeter wall, their bodies are dashed against the stones splattering the wall with blood. I search for any sign of Mara. The castle has been breached. *Where are Grandfather and Mother? Have they fled to safety, forced to abandon their beloved home?*

The incinerating heat from the flames in the courtyard have driven the remaining troops out. Hot ash rains down like gray snow. I raise my head above the billowing clouds of smoke in search of any signs of life in the Black Keep. A scream cuts through the night. I see a woman dangling from a balcony to my left, one of the hand maids. A figure dressed in black robes grasps the front of her dress. The hooded figure catches sight of me, I cannot see a face but, I feel my blood run cold. The intruder suddenly releases the maid who plummets like a stone. I lunge forward to catch the shrieking woman, she lands on my back. I crouch down so that she can slide safely to the ground.

"Oh thank you! Bless you, sweet creature!"

She takes off running towards the west gate. I look back up to the balcony to see the cloaked figure has vanished. The clash of steel sounds behind me. I brace for another wave of invaders. Rowan bursts through the flames with Terra and Xavier on his heels. He looks both irritated and relieved to see me. I close my eyes and transform back to my human form. My body is getting used to shifting between forms. There is hardly any pain as I shrink back down to the earth.

"Well done, catching up," Rowan says.

"I knew you would be opposed to my coming," I say defensively.

"I'm just glad you're safe," Rowan says tiredly. "Have you found any survivors?"

"A hand maid. Someone dressed in black robes tossed her over the balcony just there. I did not get a glimpse of a face."

"Let's search the Black Keep," Xavier says.

"They may be barricaded in one of the secret rooms."

Rowan and Xavier take point as we move into the castle. Terra and I watch our rear. The great hall is in ruins. The floor to ceiling windows are shattered, the floor splattered with blood, wood splinters from broken tables and chairs are scattered about, and the throne has been set on fire.

"Vatn," Terra speaks as she extends a hand toward the burning throne. A stream of water shoots forth to douse the flames.

We head to the left of the throne to check the royal chambers. I feel like I am walking through a nightmare. I can scarcely breathe as we come upon my Mother's chamber where her door hangs off its hinges. The room has been ransacked, clothes, books, jewelry, and linens are strewn on the floor. I stumble out and head for Grandfather's chambers. Rowan is at my side saying something to comfort me but, his words are drowned out by the blood pounding in my ears. Grandfather's chambers are in the same state of disarray. I move further into the room and nearly trip over a still form on the floor. A cry escapes me as I fall to my knees and pull my Mother's head into my lap. Her chest is still rising, her breath coming in shallow gasps. She opens her eyes and smiles at me.

"Hello, little bird," she whispers, reaching a bloodied hand up to my face.

"I'm here. I've got you," I say as tears stream down my face, making my voice thick with emotion.

I press my hand over a deep wound in her abdomen. Rowan kneels down and gently removes my hand so he can working his healing magick. He closes his eyes and presses his palms down. I watch the crease between his brows deepen, a sheen of sweat dampens his forehead from the effort. My Mother gazes up at me.

"I love you, Io. You will be a fine Queen. Do not be afraid."

She smiles as her eyes flutter closed, her

hand slips from my cheek. Her chest falls and does not rise. Rowan looks up to me, his face etched with sorrow.

"Mother? Come back! Please, don't go," I plead as hot tears trail down my ash covered face.

Terra and Xavier appear in the door way. "We found the King. He is asking for you, Io."

I am numb. I barely register Terra's words. Rowan helps me to my feet. We follow Terra and Xavier to the library where a group of Kingsguard and castle staff are gathered around the hearth. As we approach all eyes turn to us. Grandfather is seated in an arm chair, his pale face etched with pain. Bloody bandages wrap his torso. I swallow a lump in my throat as I kneel before him.

"Mother is gone," I say as flatly.

Grandfather takes my hand in his. My heart sinks when I feel his cold skin. *Are you going to leave me too?* He meets my gaze with those warm brown eyes.

"I feared the worst when I could not find

her," he says with tears glimmering in his eyes.

"We will rise from the ashes and repay the violence our enemies dealt, tenfold," I say fiercely.

Grandfather squeezes my hand. He pushes up from his chair, I help him rise. He turns to address the survivors.

"You have all fought valiantly to defend our home. Some gave their lives for our beloved kingdom. We will burn their bodies so their souls will be at peace. Tend to the wounded, offer kindness and help to all who need it. We will prepare meals and set up shelters."

Grandfather's advisors move forward to receive their orders. I step aside to make way for them. Rowan's mother, Selene, embraces each of us before heading back to the infirmary to tend to the wounded. Rowan takes me by the hand and leads me away. We find Terra and Xavier waiting in the corridor.

"I'll collect wood for the pyres," Xavier volunteers.

"I'll help you," Rowan offers.

"I will see what we can prepare in the kitchens," Terra says. "Do you want to give me a hand, Io?"

I nod. Rowan gives me a kiss. "I'll check on you shortly."

I give him a small smile. Terra and I are surprised to find the kitchens untouched. *Some luck at last.* We find some roast chickens in the pantry, carrots, onions, celery, and potatoes. We decide on chicken soup. As we are chopping vegetables, Felix walks in. His left forearm is bandaged and he looks shaken but, otherwise unharmed.

"Mind if I join you?"

"Happy to have you," I say with a smile. "We can use your expert culinary skills."

Felix washes his hands and starts shredding the roast chickens for soup. I am glad to have a task to keep my grief at bay. When Felix finishes with the chicken he moves onto preparing bread dough. Terra fills a large cauldron in the hearth with water and adds the chicken bones to make a broth. She arranges logs and kindling under the cauldron. She whispers a spell to summon flames, in no time the crackling fire starts to heat the cauldron. The savory aroma calms me. I finish chopping the carrots, onion, and celery. Terra joins me in peeling potatoes.

"Are you alright?"

"Yes, I am alright," I say, offering her a weak smile.

"Your Mother was a brave woman, Io. I know you will make her and your Grandfather proud. We will get through this. I will stand with you, Sister."

"Thank you, Terra," I say, wiping away a tear.

"Chin up, Love," Terra says wrapping an arm around me.

Rowan walks in. Our eyes meet and I feel tears welling up again. He crosses then kitchen and picks up a potato.

"Alright there, Felix?"

"I've still got some fight in me," Felix says with a wink.

In that moment I take a deep breath. *This is not the time for tears. Mara has drawn first blood. We will answer in kind. Elaria is in my sights. Blood will flow and Fire will reign.*

12

MARA

"Tell me where she is!?"

"I-I do not know! Please, have mercy!"

The blubbering girl is trying my patience. I sneer as she stares at me with wide terror-filled eyes. I strike her across the face, knocking her to the floor. She sobs, clutching her red cheek. I seize the front of her thread bare shift and drag her to the balcony. I shove her over and she screams. The sound brings a smile to my lips.

"Do you know where the Princess is now?" I ask sweetly.

I watch with disgust as the wretch wets herself. Her fingers dig into my sleeve. I glance down and see the very person I have been searching for, *Io. She does make a rather fetching Dragon.* I smile at my sweet little sister as I release her pretty little maid. She shrieks as she careens toward her death. Io rushes to the rescue. I sweep back inside. Brigid is nearly dead, bleeding all over the carpet.

"Your daughter has returned home. A pity she was late," I whisper in her ear.

"She will kill you for this," Brigid says, gazing into my eyes.

She extends her palm, the wooden chair next to her sprouts twisting vines. The vines shoot at me. I hold my palm out and freeze them. I clench my fist and the vines wither. They fall to the carpet in a shriveled heap.

A flicker of fear gnaws at me. I stamp it down. "I believe I will be sending her to you."

I give her a vicious kick. She groans and

clutches at her abdomen. I reach down and yank my dagger free. Brigid gasps as blood spills from her lips.

"Bitch!"

"Oh come now, is that anyway to speak to a Queen?"

"You are no Queen."

"It seems you won't be," I say with a peel of laughter.

I step over her and leave her to die. *Maybe if you hurry you can kiss mummy good-bye, Io.* I take a left out of the King's chambers and make my way to the library. The hand maid said there was a secret passageway near the hearth. I find the sconce next to the suit of armor and pull. I slip into the tunnel. When I emerge from the beach side cave, the Goddess Hel is waiting for me.

"Well done, Mara. You are becoming a force to be reckoned with, my dear."

"Thank you, Goddess," I say bowing my head.

Half of her face is youthful and lovely, the

other half is sunken and decaying. The living half of her body has pristine cream colored skin. The dead half is tinged blue with the pallor of death. She glides over and places a pale hand beneath my chin. She gently tips my chin up so that I can meet her grey eyes.

"You are blossoming into a radiant Mage, my daughter. It is almost time to show our hand. You have the Dragon's attention. She will come and we will slay her."

"Why is she so important?"

"A Dragon's heart contains powerful magick. Magick that will turn the tides in our favor. Magick that can grant your every desire. What is it that you desire, Mara?"

"I want-" I hesitate, touching a trembling hand to my chest. "My home restored, love, and family."

"Ah, such a mortal desire," the Goddess of the Death laughs, regarding me with cold grey eyes. "You are so young, my sweet love."

"What is it that a Goddess desires?"

She touches my cheek with a slender finger, her pink and blue lips curving up into a broad smile. "Power over all the realms. Gods and Goddesses kneeling at my feet. Mortals worshipping me as the one true Goddess."

Her eyes have a faraway look to them, her voice a maniacal tone that makes me shiver. When she turns her gaze back to me, I smile obediently. She kisses my cheek and offers me her hand. I place my hand in hers. With a snap of her fingers, we vanish from the rocky shores of Caelen. I squeeze my eyes shut as we fly through a dark void. She calls this place 'the in between.' The air is frigid. The wind rushes in my ears. Pain shoots through me as my feet slam into the ground. When I open my eyes, I am standing in my room at Castle Greenwood.

"Good night, my darling. Give the Prince a kiss for me."

Hel flicks her wrist and a swirling vortex opens on my chamber wall. She steps through, leaving me alone. I drop into a chair and hug myself as a wave of nausea crashes over me. I have been feeling sick lately and portal traveling does not help. I wretch violently into the bucket by my bedside table. I dab sweat from my brow as I struggle to catch my breath.

"Mara?"

I look up to see Richard, Prince of Arrow. We have been betrothed since birth. His family have been instrumental in the restoration of Elaria. He crosses the room in quick strides and kneels in front of me, his face etched with concern.

"Richard, please. I don't want you to see me like this," I protest.

"Mara you are unwell. You need a healer."

He kisses me and stands. "Here drink some water," he says offering me a cup from the nightstand. "I will send for Lady Gwen."

"Thank you, my love."

Richard helps me to the bed. I close my eyes and fall into a restless sleep. I dream of a burning field. The smoke chokes me. I claw at my throat as my lungs burn for air. I fall to my knees. Golden eyes glare at me through the fire and smoke. Colossal jaws open and I am engulfed in flames. I scream until my raw throat bleeds and my voice gives out. I writhe in agony.

"Mara!"

I open my eyes and Richard is holding my hand. Lady Gwen is standing next to him, peering at me with concern.

"Are you alright, Princess?"

"Just a bad dream," I say, brushing the hair from my face.

I am drenched in sweat. My gown clings to me uncomfortably. I sit up. Richard rubs my back. I lean my forehead against his shoulder.

"The Prince tells me you are unwell. When did the vomiting start?"

"Four months ago," I say, glancing at Richard guiltily.

He gives me a disappointed look. I did not want to bother him with it. We have both been so busy with our royal duties and wedding plans. I attributed my queasy stomach and interrupted moon cycle to stress.

"Please lie back and lift your dress," Lady Gwen says as she washes her hands at the basin.

Richard gives my hand a gentle squeeze as I lie back. I can feel my heart racing as Lady Gwen takes a seat on the bed. She gently spreads my legs. I can feel my knees trembling as she performs a pelvic exam. I feel like I am going to vomit again.

"Princess, you are pregnant," Lady Gwen says with a warm smile.

I lurch over the side of the bed and vomit. Richard holds my hair for me as I empty my stomach. He helps me lie back against the pillows. I feel like I may faint.

"Oh Mara," Richard says, kissing me. "This is wonderful news!"

"I-I can't believe this," I say, clutching my roiling stomach.

"It is alright, my dear. Women have babies everyday. We have the finest Midwives in

Elaria. You are in good hands, Princess. I'll give you two some privacy. I'll be back in a few days to check on you."

Lady Gwen rises. Richard walks her to the door. When he returns, he smiles at me. He places a gentle hand on my belly.

"I know this was unexpected. How are you?"

"I can't do this," I say, panic rising. "I cannot be a Mother."

I jump to my feet and start pacing. Richard pulls me into his arms.

"Mara, everything is going to be alright. I am going to take care of you and baby."

My knees give out and Richard scoops me into his arms. He lays me gently on the bed, smoothing my hair as the tears fall. When I calm down, I turn my face up to his.

"You are truly happy about this?"

"Of course! Mara, I love you."

Tears flow freely as I launch myself into his arms. I cling to him like a frightened child. I fear that this impending war will rob me of my chance at a happy life. The pain that I have inflicted will be repaid. *I fear I have strayed too far into the darkness to find my way back to the light.*

"I love you," I whisper against his lips.

I push away my worries and give myself to him. The man who does not see the monster but, the woman beneath. I have to win this war so that we can have a life of peace. I will fight for him and our child. I will create a new world where we can live without fear. A world without magick, where all people are equal.

13

MARA

"Clear your mind. Focus your energy."

A flicker of irritation flares inside me as I adjust my stance. I nod that I am ready. Hel sends a fireball at me, I brace and extend my right palm out to cast my forcefield. A blue light surrounds me, the fire crashes against my forcefield but, is unable to penetrate.

"Ah! Some progress at last!"

I lower my arm, as exhaustion sets in. Hel embraces me and kisses my forehead.

"Come, rest now," she says guiding me to a chair. "You must not over exert yourself. It is not good for baby."

She gently pats my growing belly with a smile. I still fear becoming a mother amidst all this chaos. *How can I bring an innocent into this world?* Surely my sins will taint such a pure soul. *I am no mother.*

"Let us conclude for the day. You need your rest."

"Thank you, Goddess. You do me a great kindness."

"You have proved yourself worthy of my benevolence. Do not be troubled. All is going according to plan. You will bring this baby into a new world."

Hel fades into the shadows of my chamber. I close my eyes as I exhale. Our spy reports that King Eamon is gathering troops from neighboring lands. No news on the Princess. *What are you up to, Io?*

"How was your lesson?"

I open my eyes to see Richard in the doorway. I smile and rise to meet him. He greets me with a kiss.

"Exhausting," I say.

"I can see that. Let's get you some food."

We go down to the kitchens. I cannot walk into the kitchens without memories of Io flooding my mind. I think of the last time we were here together, the day Caelen attacked. *Brigid gave us apples. Does Io know that she died by my hand?*

War gives good people the justification to commit murder in the name of a cause. But when the battle is won, when the 'evil' is defeated, how do we live with ourselves? How do we mend our souls? When is it safe to stop looking over our shoulders?

I often wonder what would have come next if the Goddess Hel had not found me that day in the woods as I lay dying. I close my eyes and replay that fateful day.

Someone is screaming. I am so weak from blood loss that I cannot open my eyes. It won't be long now. My brief life is coming to a violent end.

I can barely feel the pain anymore. All I feel is the cold icy grip of death, pulling me down.

"What a pretty thing you are. Such a waste."

I manage to peer beneath my lashes. Terror seizes me as I take in the woman before me. Half of her body is glowing with youth and vitality. The other half is withered and decaying like a corpse. She is a Goddess of the Underworld.

"I am the Goddess Hel. I have come to save you, Princess."

"Why?" I croak.

"I sense great power within you, my child. A spark that I intend to nurture. If I restore your life, will you help me?"

"What must I do?"

"Anything I ask," she says with a mischievous smile.

I shiver as I stare at her collapsed cheek and cavernous eye socket. This feels like a trick. I should refuse. But I fear death. I am not ready to go.

"I will obey," I rasp.

The Goddess presses her lovely pale hand to

my chest. I cry out as a searing heat flares within me. I gasp for breath. The heat fades and I feel no pain. I sit up and inspect my wound. It has healed completely. I feel strong. I stand.

"Feeling better?" She asks with a gruesome grin.

"Much better. Thank you. What must I do?"

"I will come to you when I am in need of your help. Rest now, my daughter."

I shake my head as I come back to the present. Richard offers me a plate of stew and fresh baked bread. We take our meals back to my chambers. I have no appetite but, I force feed myself half of the plate so Richard won't worry. We sit by the hearth when we are through, sipping tea. I rub my belly. *Please do not take this blessing from me. Please do not take Richard from me.* I don't deserve mercy but, I pray for it anyway.

14

MARA

When I wake, Richard is getting dressed. He smiles down at me.

"I tried not to wake you."

"I am glad I can send you off with a kiss."

He leans down and I bring my lips to his. He always rises early to head down to the armory. He trains the young knights alongside the Master at Arms. I keep myself busy around the castle. When I can escape my Mother's notice, I meet with Hel in secret to learn magick. Richard has met her a few times, walking in on our lessons by accident.

He was alarmed at first and rushed to my defense. This greatly amused the Goddess and she has grown quite fond of my Prince.

"Be careful today. I worry that she is pushing you too hard."

"I will be careful. I promise."

"What are her plans? I fear that she is not being forthcoming."

"I must obey. I have no choice. She saved my life, Richard."

"I don't want to lose you, Mara. I will do everything in my power to keep you safe."

I wrap my arms around his neck, he takes me into his arms. My heart races at the thought of losing the one person who truly cares for me. I feel like time is slipping away. I have a terrible feeling that this world will tear us apart.

"We should run," he says. "I will not lose you. We can leave just before dawn, ride far away from here. Find a safe place to raise our family."

"I might be able to sleep at night knowing

that we are far from this war. But she will find me. She will punish me for running."

"I will take your place. I will do as she asks."

"No. You go and find us a new home. When this is over. I will find you."

"I will not leave you alone with her. We'll finish this together."

"I do not deserve you, Richard. You are an honorable man, kind and brave. You have worked your way into my black heart."

"I will not hear such nonsense. You are my love, the mother of my child. I will keep you and our baby safe."

My cheeks are wet with tears of joy. Richard gazes into my eyes.

"Promise me that you will not do anything reckless? We are in this together."

"I promise," I say, swallowing a lump in my throat.

Richard stares right into my very soul. If he does not believe me, he shows no sign of doubt. I do not want to lie, I keep no secrets from Richard. But the thought of losing him because of my involvement with dark forces is more than I can bear. If it comes to it, I will do everything in my power to save him. Even if that means we do not get the happily ever after I yearn for.

After Richard leaves for the morning, I dress and clean my teeth. I wash my face and brush my hair. The dress makers have brought up some lovely gowns that accommodate my growing belly. I select a ravishing violet gown with golden embellishments. I head to the woods to clear my head. It seems like just yesterday I walked this path looking for Io. I stop at her favorite tree. I place a hand on the bark and close my eyes. Io's face appears in my mind. *How can it be that two years have passed since that day?*

"It is not wise to dwell on the past, my darling."

I jump and turn to see the Goddess watching me with a sad smile.

"It is hard not to think of her here."

"I understand. I have witnessed centuries of pain and loss. This will all be over soon. Then you can live in peace."

"I am not sure that I will be able to live with myself. Who am I to take her life? Perhaps she has a love? Dreams of starting a family? How can I rob her of that?"

"War is an ugly business. If you want to win, you need to sacrifice part of your very soul to do what others will not."

Hel regards me with grey eyes, her face half heaven and half hell. I nod my understanding. She holds her arms out. Her whole, unblemished hand holds a red rose. Her skeletal, decaying hand grips the hilt of a magnificent obsidian sword.

"A rose to cast on your pyre? Or a sword to avenge your Kingdom?"

She regards me with her cool gaze. Her calm countenance masks the simmering rage beneath the surface. *I have sold my soul. I am in her debt. She gave me life when I was a breath from death, she can easily take it away.* I step forward and reach for the sword. The Goddess passes it to me with an appraising smile. I grip the hilt tightly, the pain of the metal biting into my flesh sharpens my resolve.

"Let's finish this."

"Spoken like a true Queen."

Hel turns the rose to ash, the wind carries it away. A shiver runs down my spine. Anxiety turns my stomach. *I am lost. Doomed to carry out the Goddess of Death's bidding.*

"Do not look so grim, Mara. You will have a place by my side when I rise to power. All beings, Divine and Mortal will answer to me. You will rule Veridian for me. You will have everything you desire."

"I only desire a quiet life with my family. Peace after the blood shed, a second chance at life."

"And you shall have it, my daughter. Come, there is much to be done. Time to remind our enemies who they are dealing with. First we must teach them to fear us. Once we have broken their spirits, we will offer them hope through acts of kindness. It will take time to earn their trust and generations to earn their love. No matter, our game is long."

Hel casts her arm in a circle, opening a swirling portal. She extends her hand to me. I place my hand in hers and we step through. I squeeze my eyes shut as wind whips past my face, filling my ears with a dull roar. I grip Hel's hand tightly. I sway as I feel my feet touch solid ground again. When I open my eyes, we are standing on the edge of a village I do not recognize.

"Where are we?"

"This is Farrow, a village not far from the Black Keep. We will make an example of them."

My palms become slick with sweat and my breathing grows ragged. I push my nerves away. *Do not look weak. It must be done.*

"This is one of the many villages here in Caelen that is home to mages, elementals, and magickal creatures. Under our rule, magick is a privilege, not a right. All magickal beings will be under our control."

"What would you have me do?"

"Show them the cost of disobedience. Kill them all. Burn the village to the ground."

My heart shatters. I grip the sword in my hand and nod. Hel leads the way into the village. Children run at the sight of her. Mothers usher frightened children inside and bar their doors. Hel raises her hands above her head, the sky is blotted out by swirling violet clouds. Thunder booms, the ground trembles beneath our feet, and blue lightning crackles. She sets her sights on a farmer with a pitch fork. She sends a blue bolt of lightning at him. It hits him square in the chest, stopping his heart. His body crumples. A group of women drawing water up from the well take off, screaming as they run for their lives. Hel sends a violet fireball after them. The women are incinerated.

"Don't be shy, Mara. Show them what you can do."

I conjure a ball of violet fire and cast it at the meeting house in the town square. The flames engulf the thatch roof. The fire quickly spreads to the shops. The villagers flee in terror. No one stands against us. The village consists of farmers, seamstresses, bakers, inn keeps, shop keepers, elders, women, and children. I see a little girl crying in the middle of the street, she is looking for someone. My instinct is to run to her. Hel opens her arms, sending bolts of brilliant blue lightning down on the village. The little girl is struck by a bolt. She is thrown backward. Her skin blistered from the searing heat. Her little body lies still. She clutches a doll to her chest. I stifle the rising sob in my chest.

I lock my heart away. I step forward and open my arms, the ground shifts beneath our feet. A deep rumble that rattles my bones. Large cracks open up in the packed earth. Homes crumble, people are knocked off their feet as the ground ripples like a wave at sea. Geysers of hot molten earth spew forth, setting fire to the remaining structures. The smell of burnt flesh turns my stomach. The village is in ruins, bodies litter the cracked earth. The sobs and screams of survivors fill the air. A woman buries her face in the chest of her fallen lover, I feel her excruciating pain as I watch her throw her head back and scream. I tear my eyes away.

"Extraordinary. Fine work, Mara. Now we let the rest live so they can spread the story."

Hel turns away from the chaos and opens another portal. I step through without a word. I feel hollow. The sound of their screams echo in my ears long after we are whisked away from the dead and the grief stricken loved ones they left behind. Hel embraces me when we set foot back in the forest.

"Get some rest, my darling. You look unwell."

"I am just tired from our travels. Please excuse me."

"Of course my dear. Sleep well."

Hel slips into the shadows beyond the

trees. A breeze carries her scent of dahlias and decay. I walk back to the castle. The sun is low in the sky. Richard will be returning soon. I walk back to my chambers in a trance, scarcely seeing my surroundings. When I close the door behind me, I collapse onto the floor and weep. When my tears are spent, I drag myself over to the hearth and fall asleep before the fire.

15

MARA

I groan as a knock at the door rouses me from my sleep. I smooth the wrinkles from my dress and attempt to tame my hair as I walk to the door. I pull it open and stare at the woman on the other side, she is tall and lean with long red hair, dressed in a hand maid's simple pale green gown.

"I beg your pardon, Your Grace," she says bowing deeply. "My name is Willow, I am your new hand maid."

"What happened to Dara?" I ask suspiciously.

"She is with child, Your Grace. She has gone to live with her family until the babe arrives."

"Very well. Pleased to meet you, Willow. Apologies, I was unaware of Dara's condition."

"It was unexpected. She asked me to pass on her apologies. She has been having a hard time carrying out her duties."

"Please see to it that she has everything she needs. She was always very kind to me."

"Of course, Your Grace. That is most generous of you. Is there anything else you need of me at this time?"

"No, thank you, Willow. Please go take your supper."

"Thank you, Your Grace. I will be back to check on you in the morning."

Lady Willow bows and takes her leave. *Strange. I did not know that Dara had a lover.* I dismiss my suspicions. She was my hand maid after all not my friend. It is silly of me to think that she would freely share the intimate details of her life with a royal. I take a seat at my vanity and run a brush through my hair. I wash my face at the wash basin and grab my cloak. Rowan must have gotten tied up at the training yard. I head out to look for him.

I step out into the courtyard, the sun setting and the air has cooled considerably. I am glad that I remembered my cloak. I cross the courtyard to the armory. The guards nod as I make my way to the training yard beyond. I can hear the usual grunts and clashes of steel as I approach. Richard is sparing with a young knight. Sir Alan Grim, the Master at Arms is instructing a group of knights on the basics of swordsmanship nearby. I watch from the viewing platform as Richard blocks a strike from the eager young knight.

A loud explosion from the courtyard rocks the viewing platform and I am knocked backward into the wall. The air rushes from my lungs, I blink to clear my blurred vision as my ears ring. Shouts rise from the training yard as the knights scramble to render aid. I push myself up and stagger down the steps.

"Princess, come with me. It is not safe here," a dark haired knight says leading me away from the path back to the courtyard.

We freeze as a thunderous roar sounds in the courtyard. Screams pierce my ears. A terrified servant girl comes flying around the corner, the hem of her dress singed. The valiant young knight springs into action, steering me down a side corridor leading to the cellars. A stream of women and children are flowing toward the safety of the cellars.

"You'll be safe here, Princess."

"Thank you, good Sir," I say studying his handsome face with deep green eyes, he can be no more than sixteen.

He gives me a nod before dashing off to help his brothers in arms. *Goddess protect him.* I wait until he is out of sight to slip from the cellar. I race back toward the training yard. Another roar rattles my bones as I run past knights with swords in hand. I climb the stairs to the battlements. I gulp down a lungful of air as I set foot on the landing. My heart seizes as I take in the scene of the courtyard below. Elaria and Caelen forces are fighting to the death. The clashing of steel sets my teeth on edge. A dragon, black as a starless night towers over them all, spewing fire. I hold my arms out and turn my face skyward. I call forth a vicious storm, the clouds sweep in, plunging us into darkness. Thunder booms over the battle and blue lightning crackles from my fingertips. I send a bolt at Io, hitting her in the torso, she roars and sways, knocking into the side of the castle, sending a cascade of stone down on the men and women fighting in the courtyard. A few unfortunate souls are crushed under the falling hunks of stone, blood oozes from beneath them.

Io recovers, turning her face skyward. We lock eyes and I dive to my right to avoid a stream of fire. I flatten myself to the flagstone, the searing heat from the flames blisters my shoulder. I grit my teeth and drag myself back to the stairs. The battlements tremble as Io lands heavily mere feet from me. I scramble to my feet and dash down the stairs, a wall of fire pursuing my frantic steps. I crash into the side of the corridor as I narrowly escape being roasted alive. I place a hand on my belly and catch my breath.

"It seems we have lured our dragon to our door," Hel says causing me to jump at her sudden appearance.

"Indeed. Now what?"

"We draw her away from the protection of her soldiers. Bring her to the forest. I'll do the rest."

I nod and make my way around the courtyard through a servant's passage. I enter the great hall, it is deserted. All the castle guards have been called to fight. My family, no doubt is hiding in the royal catacombs. My thoughts turn to Richard. *Goddess protect him.* I cross the hall, following the corridor to the kitchens where I can slip out to the gardens. My heart hammers in my chest. *This will all be over soon. Get her to the woods.*

When I step outside I send a bolt of blue lightning up into the air. I hear the beating of wings. I run for the tree line, casting bolts above me. The ground shakes as Io touches down. I weave through the trees to avoid her fire. Our beloved woods are burning around me, black smoke clouds my vision. I press onward, navigating the forest by memory. I dive beneath a blackberry bush. I peer through the leaves as I struggle to slow my breathing.

A sudden sharp pain in my belly makes me cry out. I squeeze my eyes shut and breathe deeply. *No, not now.* I crawl deeper into the forest, my panic rising as the gravity of my situation sets in. I have to find Richard. We need to flee this cursed place. I sob as I feel the gush of my water breaking. I drag myself through the underbrush, frantically looking over my shoulder for any sign of Io. A flicker of movement on my right catches my eye, a raven tangled in the brambles, desperately trying to free herself.

"Easy. Let me help you," I whisper to her.

I gently place my hand on her body and close my eyes. I can sense her fear. I reach into her mind. I show her Richard's face. She is puzzled.

"I will set you free. In return, will you find Richard? Please bring him to me," I whisper.

The raven looks at me and quarks her understanding. I carefully extract her from the tangle of thorns and vines.

"Here take this," I say tying my necklace around her leg. "Please hurry."

I release her and she flies back toward the castle. A fleeting hope. Another contraction doubles me over and I clamp my hand over my mouth to keep quiet. A rustling behind me freezes me with fear. I flatten myself to the ground. A shadowy silhouette, shrouded by smoke. I draw a dagger from my belt. As the smoke clears, I see Io's face. Golden flames caress her slender fingers and her eyes glow like embers. She is terrifying to behold. Panic grips me.

"It is an honor to meet you at last, Princess," Hel says sweetly from the shadows.

Io tenses as the Goddess steps into the clearing. Io's flames flare as she takes in Hel's terrible beauty. Hel positions herself between us to shield me from Io's notice. I drag myself silently away, deeper into the forest's embrace.

"Mara's Mistress?"

"I am the Goddess Hel. I spared Mara from death two years past when Caelen attacked Elaria."

"Ah, so she is in your debt. You are using her to achieve, what end exactly?"

"Straight to the point," Hel chuckles. "I do love a woman who means business. You have something I desire, Io."

"And what is that?"

"Your Dragon Heart," Hel smiles malevolently.

"Come and get it," Io says with menace.

I can hear the clear ring of steel as she unsheathes her sword. *Run, Io.* I hear Hel's lightning crackle. I forget my desperation to flee and watch with bated breath. Io passes her hand over her sword, coating it in her golden flames. I see a flash of green at her throat, a glowing amulet. Hel hurls a bolt of lightning at Io who knocks it away easily with her blazing golden sword. Io runs at Hel, bringing the sword down with impossible speed. Hel sidesteps the attack but, Io's sword leaves a long red slash down Hel's living cheek. Hel's face settles into a snarl as she touches her living palm to the wound.

"Impressive. That is a fine amulet. I have seen it once before. Around the neck of the Goddess of the Crossroads. Hekate, don't be shy! Come on out. It's been an age!"

A lone figure bearing a burning torch approaches the clearing. Hel's eyes glimmer with devilish delight. Hekate emerges from the trees flanked by two massive black dogs.

She regards Hel with piercing amber eyes, a ghost of a smile on her lips.

“It has indeed been an age. What havoc have you been wreaking in this realm? You have no business here, Goddess of the Underworld. You over step.”

“Why should I be condemned to rot beyond the veil? I have devoted my existence to ferrying the departed down the river. I watch as Gods and Goddesses receive their tributes, influence the mortal world, and inspire legends and songs. Now it is my turn.” Hel says with quiet violence.

“Your ill intent and lust for power will cost you. You cannot change fate. What is written will be. By interfering, you will cause only pain and suffering.”

“Keep your admonishments for your mortals.”

“You spared her but, you have only prolonged her fate. You should have kept to your realm. Now I have been sent to clean up your mess.”

Hekate turns to Io. “Io, Mara is in need of your help. Go to her,” she says firmly.

Io nods and sheathes her sword. I watch as my old friend approaches me. She kneels down beside me and takes my hand in hers. Tears betray me, flowing freely down my cheeks. Io gives my hand a gentle squeeze.

16

IO

"I've got you, Mara. Just breathe."

Mara closes her eyes and squeezes my hand. Her contractions have intensified. Baby will be here soon. Heavy footfalls and the snapping of twigs have me on my feet, gripping the hilt of my sword. A tall man with dark brown hair, a bearded face, and dark blue eyes bursts through the trees.

"Richard!" Mara gasps.

He sidesteps me and kneels at Mara's side. "I'm here," he says tenderly kissing her forehead.

I notice he is bloodied and battle weary. The way he tends to her warms my heart. I am glad that they found each other.

"Let's get you somewhere safe."

"It is too late to move her. The babe is coming," I warn.

"Thank you for caring for her," he says, turning to face me.

I merely nod and step away to allow them their privacy. A crackle of lightning draws my gaze back to where Hel and Hekate were. I creep closer to watch.

Hekate flicks her wrist, her torch vanishes. Her great hounds circle Hel, growling as they bare their teeth. Hekate casts her arms in an arc, surrounding herself with a violet force-field. Hel's blue lightning ricochets off, narrowly missing her as it rebounds. Hel growls and stomps her skeletal foot, the ground trembles beneath my feet. I jump to my left as a huge fissure opens up, cutting me off from the warring Goddesses. I run back to check on

Mara and Richard. Mara is deathly pale and exhausted. Richard is whispering softly to her, she smiles. She cries out as she gives one last push. Richard catches a beautiful baby girl, he wraps her in his cloak and places her in Mara's arms. Mara touches her little face and looks up into Richard's eyes.

"She's perfect," Mara sighs. "Hello, Ella."

"Well done, Mama," Richard says, smiling at Mara with love and admiration.

Mara looks past Richard and our eyes meet. "Thank you, Io."

"Of course," I say. "We need to get you all away from here. It is not safe."

Richard scoops Mara and baby into his arms. I cast a glance over my shoulder at the Goddesses. They seem evenly matched, their strength far from spent, if that is even possible. The four of us slip away quietly. Richard weaves through the trees. I notch an arrow and cover his back as we move as quickly as possible. Up ahead there is an ancient rusted gate concealed behind some creeping ivy. I open my mouth to tell Richard about it but, he parts the ivy curtain on his own. Mara and I used to sneak out of the castle this way as children. The passage beyond the gate is an earthen tunnel that leads to the royal catacombs where Mara's ancestors are buried. I light my palms with golden flame to light our way. Richard is strong but, I can see that he did not escape the battle without injury. He is favoring his right side, I can see blood seeping through the tunic beneath his leather jerkin. His breathing has become uneven. If I can find Rowan, he can help heal him. *Hang on, Richard.*

After an eternity we finally see the staircase up ahead that leads to the secret passage entrance behind the enormous portrait of Mara's family tree. *Mama will need to add your branch to the family tree, little Ella.* I sweep around Richard and push the heavy door open. Richard sets Mara and Ella down gently on the floor, immediately collapsing beside them.

“Richard!” Mara shrieks.

“Richard? Can you hear me?” I ask gently rolling him onto his back. Richard moans as I cut away his leather jerkin and tunic to inspect his wound. I swallow hard as I take in the damage. The cut is deep and the blood loss is severe. His skin is deathly pale, cold to the touch. Richard turns his face toward Mara. She sobs and inches closer to him.

“I love you, Mara. I will always love you and our little Princess,” he says smiling, the love in his eyes brings tears to my own.

“Richard, please don’t leave me. Please!”

Mara presses a kiss to his lips. “I love you,” she whispers so softly that I barely hear it.

Richard smiles as his eyes slip closed. His smile fades into the peaceful stillness of death. Mara screams, clutching at the sleeve of his shirt. She screams again, suddenly pushing up into a sitting position and struggling to her feet. She hugs Ella to her breast and then offers her to me.

"What are you doing?" I ask horrified.

"She will pay for this," Mara says with deadly calm. She presses a kiss to Ella's brow and then one to my cheek.

She walks off without another word. I stand dumbstruck for a moment as I watch her go.

"Mara! Mara, come back!"

I look down at the tiny baby girl nestled in her father's cloak, stained with her parents' blood. She has dark auburn hair. When she blinks up at me, I see Richard's eyes. She stares at me with those endless ocean eyes. I smile down at her. I kneel beside Richard, suddenly overcome by the realization that he will never see her grow up. She will never hear him laugh as he chases her through a field of wildflowers. She will never jump into his arms when he comes home. I hold her up so that she can look upon his face.

"Ella, this is your father, Richard. He loved

you and your mother very much. He would have given anything to stay with you. Don't ever forget him."

I watch her little face as she gazes at him. I swear I see her lips curve into a smile. Or perhaps it is a trick of my heart, showing me what I want to see. I place her face close to his. She lets out a small cry that breaks my battered heart. I hurry back through the secret passage. I am drenched in sweat when the ivy curtain comes into view. My heart leaps as I see Mara slipping past the ivy leaves.

"MARA!"

She does not turn back. I feel as though I might faint but, I push myself onward. *Ella cannot lose you both.* I burst through the ivy and look around wildly. Mara is moving slowly but, determinedly back toward where we last saw Hel and Hekate. My hearts stutters when I realize that she is leaving behind a trail of dark red blood. I run after her as fast as I dare, clutching tiny Ella to my chest.

Hel and Hekate are at each other's throats.

Neither one sees Mara silently approach from behind. Mara shoots her hand into Hel's skeletal rib cage and rips out a withered black heart. Hel's living eye opens wide in shock. A strangled cry escapes her lips as she loosens her grip on Hekate's throat. Hekate does not hesitate. She drives a curved obsidian dagger into Hel's living breast. She twists it savagely, bringing Hel to her knees.

"Back to the abyss, Sister," Hekate purrs.

Hel glares at Hekate as she turns to gray ash. Mara collapses to the ground, Hel's withered black heart disintegrates to ash in her hand, the west wind carries it away. Hekate goes to Mara's side. The ten steps I run feels like crossing a vast desert. I drop to my knees. Hekate gently rolls Mara onto her back. Mara is barely breathing.

"Mara!"

Her eyes open, the very effort seems to drain her even further. I place Ella in her arms. Mara holds her tightly, a single tear rolls down her left cheek. She struggles to raise Ella's face to her lips. I lift Ella gently up so that she can kiss her daughter for the last time. A sob tears out of my chest.

"I love you, Ella. I love you, Io," Mara says with a smile. "Please take care of my daughter."

The tears spill over and I hug her. Ella fusses and I draw away immediately. I look to Mara's face and she is gone. Her green eyes are frozen, reflecting the forest's green canopy, tinged gold in the light of the dying sun. *I lost you twice.*

"I am sorry for your loss, Io," Hekate says, making me jolt.

I did not realize she was still here. Hekate gathers Mara into her arms.

"I will carry her to Richard in the afterlife," Hekate says solemnly. "What of the babe?"

"I will take her home," I say. "I will raise her as my own."

"Bless you, Dragon Queen. Until we meet again."

"Thank you, Hekate."

Hekate smiles before she turns away. A bright swirling indigo cloud appears before her and she steps through with Mara cradled in her arms. *Goodbye, sister.*

"IO!"

"Rowan?"

"IO!"

I turn to see him sprinting toward me. I smile as he stops short when he catches sight of the tiny bundle in my arms.

"Not ours," I say with a shake of the head.

The color slowly returns to Rowan's cheeks as he exhales.

"I was concerned," he says with a chuckle.

"She is Mara and Richard's daughter. This is Ella. Mara and Richard-" my voice cracks and Rowan's brow creases in sympathy.

"Io, love. I am sorry."

"We have to take her. She has no one," I whisper.

"Of course she can stay with us," Rowan says at once.

I regard him with shining tear-filled eyes. Rowan encircles my waist and pulls me close, careful to mind Ella. Rowan kisses me deeply and my legs threaten to give out. Rowan pulls me down to the ground gently. He steadies me with his strong hands, gently drawing my head to his chest, placing an arm beneath Ella's tiny body. My eyes drop closed and my exhaustion pulls me under.

BRIGHT LIGHT FILTERS in through the gap in my bedchamber curtains. I absently skim my fingers against my belly. I feel a kick against my fingers. It has been five months since we brought Ella home. She has grown into a happy little soul. I peek into her bassinet next to my side of the bed. Ella sleeps soundly, I watch the steady rise and fall of her chest. I reach in and scoop her into my arms. I nestle her against my round belly. Our baby stirs within, kicking gently to bid me good morning.

"Good morning, my loves," Richard says beside me. He stretches his arm out, drawing me close to him.

"Good morning, dear heart," I say with a sleepy smile.

I tire so easily now. Sleep eludes me at night, I toss and turn, unable to get comfortable.

Rowan takes Ella from my arms. I push the covers back and swing my legs to the floor. I wash my face and clean my teeth. I take a quick bath before selecting a red high necked dress with flowing bell sleeves. I run a brush through my hair and pull it back with a red ribbon. Rowan carries Ella after arguing that I should not have to carry two babies. We step out into a brisk spring morning. The sun feels good on my skin. I breathe in the smell of fresh rosemary and mint as we walk through the gardens. A gentle breeze greets us as we approach Terra's sea cliff cottage. I knock on the door. A moment later Terra opens the door and regards us with a smile.

"Hi," I say with a wave.

"Come on in."

Xavier is brewing some tea at the hearth. "Good Morning, all. How is the little princess today?"

"She's growing like a weed," Rowan says, passing her over to a visibly uncomfortable Xavier.

"Relax, she can sense fear," I chuckle.

I glance at Terra who is staring at Xavier holding Ella with a peculiar look. I suppress a smile. *He has torn down her walls and worked his way into her heart. We might be celebrating their bundle of joy soon.* Terra takes a turn holding Ella, rocking her gently. Perhaps between all of us we can give her a happy life. Terra gasps suddenly. Xavier and Rowan look over from the hearth.

"What's wrong?" I ask.

"Ella has magick. She showed me her memories!"

"What did you see?"

"She showed me Mara and Richard. Rowan, Xavier, me and you. She is happy. She loves us," Terra says with wonder.

"Incredible. Mara must have passed her magick to Ella," Xavier says thoughtfully.

"She can communicate telepathically? That seems like strong magick," Rowan says.

"It is. I have never heard of a Mage displaying powers as an infant. We should consult Lita. Ella will need to learn to control her powers."

"She is barely five months old. We can't send her away. She needs us," I protest.

"No, I can help her here. I only want to ask Lita for guidance. I will train her when she is ready."

"Will Lita come to Caelen?"

"I will send a raven."

Ella touches Terra's face. Terra laughs. "Ella likes ravens."

I smile at our little mage. *Clever girl.* I am glad to have Terra to help Ella. Magick is second nature to her. Xavier and Rowan make some sandwiches and a platter of fruit for lunch. Terra amuses Ella by turning a daisy into a butterfly. Ella giggles and waves her tiny hands. I am grateful for this room of people I love.

17

ROWAN

Terra and Xavier offer to take Ella back to Jenny, the wet-nurse, for her feeding. Io and I take a walk through the meadow. I watch the wind sweep her raven hair over her shoulder as she gazes out to sea. She closes her eyes, breathing deeply. I stand before her and place a hand on her belly. Io places a hand over mine.

"Are you ready to meet our little prince or princess?" She asks.

"Absolutely. We are ready when you are little one."

I feel a kick and Io smiles up at me. I lean down and kiss her. Io suddenly pulls away. I see a flicker of pain in her eyes.

"You ok?"

Io sinks to the ground, clutching her belly. "Hey, I've got you. It's alright. I'm here."

"Time to call the midwife," Io gasps.

I take her hand in mine. She grasps it tightly, breathing slowly through the pain. I rub my free hand up and down her back. She presses her forehead to my chest.

"Let's get you back to the castle," I say, helping her to her feet.

Io leans heavily on me as we slowly walk back toward the castle. Io clutches my arm, pulling me to a halt.

"I can't make it," she says, swaying on the spot.

I scoop her into my arms and run back to Terra's house. I burst through the door, startling Terra who is rocking Ella by the hearth.

"What's wrong?" Terra asks at the sight of us. "Oh my gosh! Baby time."

"Xavier!"

Xavier comes rushing in from the sitting room. He runs over to help me with Io. We take her into the spare bedroom. Io has closed her eyes but, her tight grip lets me know she is still with me.

"I'll fetch the midwife," Xavier says, clapping my shoulder.

"Thank you," I say giving him a nod.

Terra sweeps in with Ella. I'll heat up some water. A warm bath might help easy the labor pains. Io opens her eyes. I smile down at her.

"I love you," she says through her pain.

"I love you. You've got this," I say kissing the back of her hand.

Io smiles up at me. She falls into a restless sleep. I rub her back and apply counter pressure to her hips. The midwife steps into the room.

"Good afternoon, Rowan. Fine day to have a baby," she says with a warm smile.

"Thank you for coming, Lady Jocelyn."

"Of course, my dear. How are you, Io?"

"Hanging in there," Io sighs.

"Let me see how things are progressing."

Lady Jocelyn checks Io. I hold Io's hand as she slowly breathes in and out.

"Good news, dear heart. Labor is progressing. Baby will be here soon. You are doing beautifully."

The hours slip by as Io's contractions steadily intensify. Every tear and moan of pain, wrenches my heart. I whisper softly to her. She nods to acknowledge me, unable to speak through the waves of pain.

"Io, time to start pushing," Lady Jocelyn says firmly. "Deep breath, now push!"

Io takes a deep breath and pushes. The air rushes out of her as she takes a rest.

"Beautiful," Lady Jocelyn encourages. "Another, just like that."

The minutes crawl by as Io struggles. Lady Jocelyn turns to me suddenly.

"Come over here, Dad. Time to meet baby."

Io pushes one final time and I catch our baby. I hold the wriggling babe up so that Io can see our son. Her eyes fill with tears.

"A healthy baby boy!" Lady Jocelyn announces.

"May we come in?" Terra calls from the kitchen.

I look to Io for approval, she nods with a tired smile.

"Yes! Come in," I call.

Terra comes in followed by an awkward Xavier cradling Ella against his chest.

"Aw you guys!" Terra says with teary eyes. "He is beautiful. What is his name?"

"Finn Garrett McGlaughlin," I say.

"Good name," Xavier approves. "Happy birthday, Finn."

Ella peers at Finn with curious dark blue eyes. Xavier steps closer so she can see him better. Finn blinks at Ella. Io smiles at the exchange.

"Seems like they are off to a good start," Io says.

"We'll let you rest," Terra says nudging Xavier out the door. "We'll take Ella up to Jenny."

"We'll bring some food and clothes back for you," Xavier says.

"Thank you, both," Io says.

Lady Jocelyn helps Io clean up and settles her back into bed. She prepares an herbal tea which she instructs me to serve Io every four hours to help her recover.

"I'll let you two get acquainted with your little man. Send for me if you need anything. Otherwise, I'll be back tomorrow morning to check on mother and baby."

"Thank you, my Lady," I say with a bow.

"My pleasure, Rowan. Take care, Io," Lady Jocelyn says warmly before taking her leave.

Io's eyes start to droop and I take Finn from her arms. She falls asleep immediately. I study Finn's little face. Thick brown hair, chubby cheeks, my nose, grey eyes. He stares up at me. I touch a finger to his cheek. He turns his face and tries to suckle it.

"I can't help you there, son. Just let mama rest for a moment."

He studies my face and I stare right back, etching this moment in my memory for all eternity. *Our son. The perfect combination of the two of us.* Finn yawns and closes his eyes.

"Exhausting business, being born," I chuckle. I stand and walk him over to the window. The clouds have covered the sun, a gust of wind rustles the sea of grass that runs to the cliffs beyond.

"You picked a fine day to be born," I say. "The heat of summer is fading. The leaves will be changing from green to orange, red, and gold."

"Fall is quite beautiful," Io says sleepily from the bed.

"You should rest," I scold.

"I'm too excited. I can't believe we have a son."

"He is rather extraordinary," I say, carrying Finn back to Io.

Io cradles Finn to her chest. I lay down

beside them, my eyes slide closed of their own accord. When I wake, the room is dark, save for a flickering fire in the hearth. Terra and Xavier laid some food out on the table on the opposite side of the room. Io sleeps soundly next to me, Finn curled up in the crook of her arm. I slip out of bed slowly, careful not to disturb them. I pour cup of water and add another log to the fire to keep the room warm. I settle down in a chair at the table. A soft knock sounds at the door.

I walk over to answer it. Terra peers at me anxiously.

"Everything ok?"

"Yes, Io and baby are asleep."

"Sorry to disturb you. I'll be right across the hall if you need anything."

"Thank you, Terra."

"Get some sleep while you can," she says.

"I will," I promise.

Terra heads to her room. When she opens her door I can hear Xavier's snoring within. I smile to myself as I close the door and return to bed. *Quite an evening.* I settle down on my side of the bed. I close my eyes and drift off.

I wake to the smell of sizzling bacon and pancakes. Io's side of the bed is empty. I slip out of bed to search for my family. When I enter the kitchen, Io is seated at the table holding Finn in her arms. Terra is flipping pancakes on the griddle over the fire. I sneak a piece of bacon from a heaping plate on the table.

"Good morning," Io says brightly.

"Good morning," I reply.

I am glad to see that several hours of sleep has done Io good. The color has returned to her cheeks and she seems stronger. Io feeds a wriggling Finn. He nuzzles against her chest as Io draws his little blanket around him. Terra brings a towering stack of pancakes to the table. Xavier walks into the kitchen with a fussing Ella.

"Good morning, all," he says sleepily.

"What is all the fuss about?" Terra asks taking Ella from Xavier.

Ella touches a small hand to Terra's face. Terra whispers to her softly and kisses her forehead. Their bond has blossomed. Terra is a natural mother. I catch Xavier watching them. He only has eyes for his girls. I am grateful that Ella is so comfortable with Terra and Xavier. Io worried about Ella feeling left out once baby arrived. I think there will be no shortage of love for little Ella.

18

IO

As Terra clears the breakfast plates away, Lady Jocelyn comes to check on us. She is glad to see that I am up and about. She examines Finn, pleased with his eager appetite. Lady Jocelyn presses on my belly and asks if I am in pain. She reminds me to take it easy and rest as often as I can for a smooth recovery. She gives me a soothing balm for Finn's bottom after I change his diapers. She even gifts him a little red woolen cap and a matching blanket.

"Thank you, Jocelyn. I could not have done it without you."

"You did beautifully, Io. Terra and Xavier have offered to take care of Ella while you and Finn get settled at the castle."

"It is no trouble at all," Terra says from across the room where she rocks Ella to sleep.

"You are too kind, my friend," I say.

"You bond with Finn. We've got Ella. We'll check on you from time to time to make sure you get enough rest."

I smile as I blink away sudden tears. Terra smiles back. My heart overflows with gratitude. Exhaustion settles in and Lady Jocelyn rushes to my rescue. She takes Finn for me.

"I'll take him to Dad so you can rest, my dear."

"Thank you," I say, she is barely out the door before I fall asleep.

When I wake up I have a terrible feeling. The sun is high in the sky and I am drenched in sweat. I slip out of bed and walk into the deserted kitchen. There is a shattered mug on the floor and a puddle of tea.

"Rowan? Terra? Xavier?"

My blood turns to ice. My heart starts to race. I dash across the kitchen and push open Terra's bedroom door. The unmade bed and empty room fuel my rising anxiety. I run outside. I feel dizzy and hot. My breath comes in ragged gasps.

"ROWAN!"

"IO!" Rowan's voice rings out across the meadow.

I spin around to see Rowan and Terra supporting a slumped Xavier. I rush forward to help. We get Xavier inside. I clear the kitchen table with a hurried swipe. Rowan and Terra ease Xavier down onto the table. Rowan places a hand on Xavier's chest, his brow furrows in concentration as he works his healing magick. Sweat beads on his forehead. Xavier breathes out a relieved sigh. Rowan exhales slowly sinking into a kitchen chair.

"What happened?" I ask, frantically looking between Terra and Rowan.

"Lady Jocelyn. She took the babies," Terra says heavily.

"What?" I rasp as the world tilts violently. Rowan takes me gently by the arm, steering me to a chair.

"When she came into the kitchen she said she was grabbing something from her bag for you. She walked into the sitting room with Finn in her arms. When she did not return, I went to check on her," Xavier says in an exhausted whisper.

"Rowan ran in to get me. He found Xavier on the floor unconscious. Lady Jocelyn must have slipped something into his drink and stolen Ella," Terra says. "We searched the castle grounds. Riders have been sent to scour the villages and the road to Elaria."

I stare at the floor as Terra's words sink in. *Gone. Stolen. Our babies. I've failed Mara and Richard. I've failed Finn.* Hot angry tears come unbidden. I dash them away. I rise to my feet and head for the door. Rowan grabs my arm before I can wrench the door off its hinges.

"Io, where are you going?"

"To find Lady Jocelyn," I say through gritted teeth.

"We'll find her together."

"We'll help," Xavier says as Terra helps him into a sitting position.

Terra dashes around the kitchen, grabbing odds and ends from the shelves. She hurries to the table with an armful of tiny bottles and herbs. Xavier places a large wooden bowl on the table. Terra fills the bowl with water. She chops herbs, crushes flower petals, and adds several mysterious liquids from an assortment of bottles. The smell is sickly sweet. The liquid takes on a violet shade, as it swirls and bubbles. All the while, Terra whispers an incantation.

"Mother, Maiden, Crone hear me in my time of need. Guide me to what has been lost. Taken at

so great a cost. A friend has turned foe. Show us now where we must go."

The violet brew bubbles violently and suddenly settles. The smooth surface shows us the seaside cliffs. A lone figure hurries along the path to the sea, nervously glancing back. A pale face is clearly visible beneath the hood of a cloak. *Lady Jocelyn.*

Xavier and Rowan spring into action. They are out the door before Terra or I can say a word. Terra places her hand on top of mine.

"We're going to get them back," she says firmly.

I simply nod. I have no idea how long we sit in restless silence. I try to stop my racing thoughts. When that fails I start pacing around the kitchen. A shout from outside freezes me in my tracks. The door bangs open. Xavier hauls in a panicked Lady Jocelyn. Rowan steps in behind them and bolts the door.

"Release me!" Lady Jocelyn shrieks, as she struggles against Xavier's iron grip.

Xavier pushes her into a chair, deftly binding her hands behind her with a length of rope. Terra slaps her hard across the face. Lady Jocelyn reels backward. Xavier holds the chair steady. When Lady Jocelyn recovers she stares daggers at Terra. She opens her mouth to speak and Terra slaps her again. A trickle of blood appears at the corner of her slack mouth.

"You will speak when spoken to, not before," Terra says with quiet violence. "Who hired you to steal the children? Honesty will save time."

"I don't know what you're-"

I kick the heel of my boot into Lady Jocelyn's stomach. Her eyes go wide in shock, the air rushes out of her in a pained groan.

"WHO!?" I roar.

"Queen Raya," Lady Jocelyn rasps.

I grab a fistful of hair and wrench her

head back. Lady Jocelyn screams in terror. I press my dagger to her throat.

“Last chance. If you lie, I will carve your heart from your chest and show it to you,” I whisper into her ear.

“Please! I speak the truth. The Queen paid me ten thousand in silver to take the babes,” she blubbers.

“Where are they now?” Terra asks sharply.

“I don’t know. I-I handed them off to a woman in a carriage. We met on the edge of town.”

“What does this woman look like?”

“She was a maid. Young with dark brown curls.”

“Let’s get on the road,” Terra says turning to Xavier.

Xavier nods, gathers his things and leaves to ready the horses. Terra unties Lady Jocelyn’s bindings. She sighs, rubbing her wrists.

“Thank you,” she breathes.

“Don’t thank me,” Terra scoffs. “You are not forgiven.”

Terra pulls Lady Jocelyn to her feet. The color drains from her face. Terra drags her toward the open door. Rowan and I follow silently.

"PLEASE! NO! I told you the truth. Have mercy!"

Terra shoves her to the ground. "It is not my mercy you should beg for," Terra snarls.

I call forth my fire. The flickering flames illuminate Lady Jocelyn's horror stricken face. She scoots backward in the grass, her legs tremble violently beneath her skirts.

"PLEASE, YOUR GRACE! HAVE MERCY!"

"Did you show my children mercy when you stole them away from their family? Your life was forfeit when you handed them over to my enemy. Now face your fate with dignity."

"NOOOOOO! PLEASE!" Lady Jocelyn shrieks.

I hurl a ball of golden fire at her. It hits her in the chest, the flames consume her. Her screams rise to a frenzied crescendo. She writhes on the ground for several agonizing minutes as her clothes burn to ash and her flesh liquifies into an acrid black puddle. I walk past without a single downward glance. Rowan and Terra flank me as we make our way to the stables where Xavier is waiting with our horses. We mount up and pursue Queen Raya's dispatched hand maid.

The countryside escapes my notice as I ride at break neck speed with the wind rushing in my ears. Rowan, Terra, and Xavier barrel along beside me. We devour the road, anyone in our path scrambles out of the way. We are halfway to Elaria, with no sign of a carriage. *Perhaps that wench lied after all.* My heart pounds in my chest as I fight to remain calm. When Castle Greenwood comes into view, my rage bubbles back to the surface. The castle gates are open wide and I ride right in without a thought. I launch out of my saddle before Ash comes to a complete stop. Castle guards approach and I transform into my dragon form. They jump back in alarm as

I roar. Their faces frozen in comical expressions of shock. Rowan, Xavier, and Terra come thundering into the courtyard before I can roast the guards alive.

"We demand an audience with Queen Raya!" Rowan shouts.

A tall guard with short cropped red hair nods shakily and retreats back to the castle in haste. The remaining three back away several paces. I snort a smoke ring in their direction. They stand their ground but, I can see them trembling. I flash my gleaming white fangs and gnash my teeth. To their relief, their captain returns with Queen Raya's advisor.

"The Queen will see you now," the advisor says with a false smile, extending a sweaty palm in the direction of the stairs.

I slip back to my human form, blowing by the Queen's servant without acknowledging his presence. Terra, Xavier, and Rowan dismount and follow. We enter the great hall which is empty except for an old couple perched on matching thrones. Queen Raya looks thinner and more severe than I remember. King Roland looks dreadful, he seems to have aged 20 years since I laid eyes on him last.

"Welcome back, Io," Queen Raya says with feigned sincerity.

"Spare me the niceties," I snap. "Where are they!?"

"Your son will be returned to you once we come to an understanding."

"You told me that both of the babes were Mara and Richard's." The King says rounding on his wife. "What have you done, woman?"

"I did what I had to!" Queen Raya shouts. "Our daughter is lost to us because she sold her soul to that She Devil! I will not lose my grandchild."

"Mara entrusted Ella to me. It was her dying wish."

"Her mind was addled. She did not know what she was saying. You are not fit to be a mother!"

I shoot a ball of golden flames at the

Queen. She throws herself to the floor to dodge the fire but, fails to escape my wrath. The flames catch her voluminous green skirts and she howls in pain as the fire singes her wrinkled flesh.

"GUARDS! SEIZE THEM!" The Queen screams as she flounders on the ground in a desperate attempt to smother the flames.

King Roland backs away from his burning Queen. He halts the guards that have come running to the Queen's aid. Terra douses the Queen with a freezing deluge. The Queen whimpers and sputters as black smoke rises from the remains of her ruined gown. Her legs are badly scorched and her face is a mask of excruciating pain.

"Send for the babies," Terra orders.

King Roland nods to the Queen's trembling advisor who hurries away at once. He returns with a pair of young maids, each carrying a swaddled babe. The maids gape openly at the Queen with wide eyes. Terra beckons the girls forward.

"Give Princess Io her son," Terra orders. "Give Princess Ella to me. Then leave this place."

The maids comply and run for their lives. The Queen clumsily arranges what is left of her gown to preserve her remaining shreds of dignity. She manages to stand and summon her most regal scowl.

"You will not leave this castle with my granddaughter," she declares.

"Enough, Raya," the King says in exasperation. "Mara entrusted the girl to Io. Honor our daughter's dying wish."

"How can you abandon your own flesh and blood?" The Queen demands. "I will not stand aside as Ella is whisked away to live amongst barbarians!"

"She's probably better off with scheming kidnappers," I drawl.

The Queen shoots me a venomous look. I gaze right back. I pass Finn to Rowan.

"You did such a fine job with your own daughter," I continue.

The Queen takes the bait. She lunges at me and I sidestep her attack, extending my right leg. The Queen crashes to the polished floor with a grunt. She gets to her knees. I draw my sword and press it to her chest before she can rise to her feet.

"We're leaving now."

I turn away from the Queen. I hear the distinct whistle of an arrow. I spin on my heel and slash the shaft before the arrow can find its mark. Rowan notches an arrow and returns fire. His arrow sinks into the archer's chest with a sickening thud. The archer pitches forward over the stone banister and plummets to the great hall floor landing in a heap mere paces from us. I turn back to the Queen and drive my sword through her heart. The Queen gasps as blood spurts from her mouth. I wrench my sword free. The Queen's lips spread into a malevolent smile. The left side of her face withers before my eyes. Her cheek collapses, her skin turns to a sickening shade of blue-grey, and her eye rots in its socket. *Hel.* The Goddess seizes my right forearm. Blue lightning erupts from her skeletal hand, blasting me backward. My sword clatters across the marble floor. The air rushes out of my lungs as land on my back.

"IO!"

I manage to push up onto my forearm. Hel raises her palm toward Rowan and Finn. My breath catches in my throat. I scramble to my feet. Blue lightning explodes from Hel's palm, streaking a deadly path toward my entire world. I don't reach them in time but, Terra does. She dives in front of Rowan and Finn. Her icy blue eyes meet mine for a brief moment before she turns them to meet her fate. She throws her arms wide casting a shimmering violet barrier of protection behind her. Terra screams as her body is electrified. She convulses as her body is ravaged. She sways, her scorched skin is blistered and bleeding. Her protective barrier flickers and fades. I feel a sharp pain in my own chest as I watch her fall. Xavier rushes forward to catch her.

I run forward and drop to my knees at Xavier's side. Terra's chest is blackened and badly burned. She lies still, her chest does not rise. Xavier cradles her tenderly to his chest. His silent tears fall onto her ashen cheek. *Hekate give me strength.* I draw my dagger from my boot. I pass my left hand over the length of the blade coating it in golden flames. *For Mara, Richard, and Terra.* I scream as I lunge at the Goddess of the Underworld, driving my dagger into her chest. Her living eye flys open, black blood dribbles down her lips.

"Impossible," she gasps.

"You will never walk this realm again. I banish you to the Underworld."

She claws at my hand but, I scream and drive the dagger deeper, twisting the hilt viciously. I notice a green glow reflected in Hel's eye. My free hand touches Runa's talisman at my throat. She said I would need it to defeat Hel. My golden flames have taken on a greenish hue. The green flames seem to be burning Hel from within. Her smooth unblemished skin erupts in hideous blisters that burst and ooze foul smelling liquid. She shrieks as she is consumed by green fire. Thick black smoke rises. I wrench my dagger free and take a step back. Rowan slips an arm around my waist, holding me tightly as we back away. My eyes water as I watch the smoke form a swirling vortex. A long scream echoes throughout the hall, chilling my blood. The smoke slowly dissipates as the hall falls silent. The still form of Queen Raya lies where Hel fell moments ago. King Roland walks over to kneel beside his Queen. He bows his head and leans down to kiss her cheek.

"You are free to go," the King says without raising his eyes. "No one will pursue you. Please take care of my Granddaughter."

He looks up to meet my eyes. Tears stream down his face. The sorrow in his grey eyes tears at my battered heart.

"I will," I vow. "Please come to Caelen to visit her often."

The old King smiles a sad smile and nods. We leave the King to mourn his Queen. Rowan and I kneel beside Xavier. I gaze down at Terra's face, so peaceful in death.

I take her hand in mine. I reach up to unfasten my cloak to wrap her body. My fingers brush against the talisman. I lift it over my head and place it on Terra's chest. *If it can kill a Goddess, maybe it can bring Terra back before she slips too far from our reach. I lay the talisman over her heart.* The green glow starts to pulse. Xavier presses a kiss to Terra's forehead. The light intensifies. We all shield our eyes. I peek through my lashes. My mouth falls open, the talisman has vanished. Terra's skin is now glowing green. We all watch as Terra heals before our eyes. Her burns smooth into fresh new skin. The color returns to her cheeks and her lips draw in a breath. Terra slowly opens her eyes. Xavier smiles down at her. She looks up puzzled.

"What did I miss?" She asks.

Xavier pulls her in for a long kiss. Rowan and I step back to give them some privacy. We tend to Ella and Finn. Rowan made them a cozy nest out of his cloak. I take Finn into my arms. He blinks up at me. I smile at him as I hold him to my breast. I rock him until he drifts off to sleep. Ella coos and waves her arms about. Rowan scoops her into his arms, rocking her gently. She smiles at him, gazing at his face with wonder. Terra and Xavier join us.

"You gave us a scare," I say.

"It takes more than a Goddess of the Underworld to do me in," Terra replies with a wink.

I notice that her icy blue eyes have flecks of green in them now. Terra holds her hand up in front of her. Green light crackles from her finger tips.

"Seems like I had a little help from my friend."

I give her a rib crushing hug. Terra squeezes me right back.

"Let's go home. I'm exhausted," Terra says with a yawn.

We return to the courtyard where our horses are grazing on some grass. We fashion baby slings from Rowan and Xavier's spare shirts. Terra secures Ella to her chest and I strap Finn to mine. We mount up and set a gentle pace back to Caelen. We ride into the early evening, crossing the border into Caelen as the sun is setting. We make camp in the same pine tree grove we stopped at when I first traveled to Caelen. *Life has changed so much in the last two years.* Xavier starts a fire. Rowan sets up our tents. I chase Terra to bed even though she argues that she is fine. I can see that she is still recovering from her brush with death. She is pale and quieter than usual. Xavier goes in to check on her.

I feed Ella and Finn by the fire. Xavier manages to snare a pair of rabbits. I skin and clean them. Rowan skewers them with an iron rod. He drives two forked steaks into the dirt on either side of the fire. The smell of roasting rabbit makes my stomach growl. I turn the spit occasionally to cook our supper. When the flesh has roasted to crisp, browned perfection, Xavier carefully lifts the iron rod away from the fire with gloved hands. He places it on a wooden cutting board to cool. Rowan carves our roasted rabbits with his hunting knife. Rowan and Xavier each take a baby so I can eat. I offer to take the first watch since I will most likely have to wake up to feed the babies anyway. Xavier takes Ella to the tent he shares with Terra. Rowan spreads his bedroll out next me and lies down beside a sleeping Finn. I add another log to the fire to keep them warm. When I start to get drowsy, I walk around the campfire to stay alert. The light of the full moon makes it easy to keep an eye on our perimeter. I listen to a wolf howl in the distance. Fireflies hover above the tall grass. A curious fox slinks over to the campfire. I toss her a piece of roasted rabbit. She snatches it and disappears back into the grass.

I wake Rowan up for his shift with a kiss. He pulls me down to the bedroll. I feel at home in his arms. He stretches his arms overhead with a yawn. He gently lays me down in his spot, tucking me in next to Finn.

"I love you," I say with a sleepy smile.

"I love you," he says. "Get some rest, dear heart."

19

ROWAN

I watch over my little family as they sleep. Io is curled around our son. She is exquisite with her cinnamon complexion, raven hair, rosy cheeks, and pink petal soft lips. Finn is the perfect balance of us. Deep brown hair, light grey eyes, and olive skin. It is nearly time for me to wake Xavier for his watch. I add another log to the fire and pop a raspberry into my mouth. The sweet juice explodes on my tongue. I stand, stretching my arms overhead as I walk over to Xavier's tent.

"Xavier," I call near the entrance.

I hear a soft groan from within. A moment later a disheveled looking Xavier emerges. His tunic is backward but, at least he has laced his boots and buckled his sword belt on.

“Morning,” Xavier says, blinking sleep from his eyes.

“Morning, sunshine,” I snigger.

Xavier stretches his arms out as we walk to the camp fire. I squat down and gather Io into my arms. Xavier gently picks up Finn and follows me to our tent. I lay Io down on our pile of furs. Xavier lays Finn next to Io.

“Thank you,” I say patting him on the shoulder.

“Of course, my friend. Good night,” Xavier says, patting my shoulder on his way out of the tent.

I kick off my boots. I quietly slip off my sword belt. I lie down next to my family. I close my eyes and drift off at once. I sleep deeply. I wake to the sound of Io singing softly to Finn.

“Little fox, little fox come out to play,

The silvery moon will light our way.

Fireflies flicker above our heads,

All babes are fast asleep in their beds.

We'll run through the meadow to the back of beyond,

And dance until a new day has dawned."

"Good morning, my love," I say.

Io smiles at me with tired eyes. "Good morning, dear heart."

"Ready to go home?"

"Absolutely," Io says.

"I'll start packing up. You rest a little longer."

Io brings her lips to mine. I breathe in her familiar scent as the world slips away. She lays down beside Finn and closes her eyes. I clean my teeth and splash some water on my face. I dress quietly. I gather up our belongings before stepping outside to ready the horses. Xavier is packing away their tent.

"Morning," he says as I emerge.

"Morning. Where are the girls?"

"They walked over to the cliffs. Ready to head out?"

"Definitely. Just letting Io get a few more minutes of sleep."

Terra walks up carrying a giggling Ella. Xavier smiles at the sight of them. *They make a lovely family.*

"Morning, ladies," I say.

"Good morning."

"I'll get the horses ready and then wake Io."

I make my way over to our mounts. Nyx whinnies as I approach.

"Let's go home, girl."

She nuzzles my shoulder as I place her blanket and saddle. Io slips up beside me, silent as a shadow. Finn peers curiously at Nyx, from the safety of his mother's arms. He reaches a tiny hand toward her. Io steps closer so he can touch Nyx's neck. Nyx turns her head to get a better look at Finn. She cautiously sniffs the top of his head. Io strokes her neck. I saddle Ash. Io greets him with a gentle stroke of his forehead. She mounts up, Finn nestled securely against her chest.

Xavier brings over our tent bundle. I strap it behind my saddle. I mount up as Terra and Ella join us. We set out as the sky is lightening to a shade of lavender. Everyone is anxious to reach Caelen. When the Black Keep comes into view we all quicken our pace. The villages are just waking up as we pass through. Women are hanging out their washing, children are collecting eggs from their chicken coops, and men are tending their fields. The smell of fresh bread wafts out the baker's window. The ring of steel sounds from the blacksmith's forge. Many people call out greetings and wave. Io graciously acknowledges every kind word, returns every wave with a smile. *They love her. She will be a beloved Queen.*

When we arrive at the Black Keep, King Eamon greets us in the courtyard.

"Welcome home. I am relieved to see you all in good health," the King says. "Please get some rest. I have asked the cooks to prepare a late supper."

"Thank you, Grandfather. It is good to be home," Io says.

She dismounts and walks forward to embrace the King. He smiles warmly as he embraces his granddaughter and great grandson. I take Ash and Nyx to the stables while Io introduces the King to Finn. I glance over my shoulder to see the King cradling our son in his arms. Terra and Xavier follow me to the stables.

"I can't wait for a hot bath," Terra sighs as she stows away Ares's saddle. She leads him to a stall with fresh water and hay. Xavier scoops Terra into his arms as she turns away from her horse. She giggles uncharacteristically. I leave them to have their moment in peace. I return to Io and the King in the courtyard.

"Rowan," the King says pulling me into an embrace. "Thank you for returning them safely to me."

"Of course, my King," I say.

“Please rest and I will see you at supper.”

Io places Finn in his cradle at our bedside. We collapse into bed, exhaling simultaneously as we sink into the soft coverlet. Io meets my eye and we laugh. I brush a strand of hair from her face, lightly trailing the tips of my fingers down her cheek. I lose myself in those deep brown eyes, like fresh turned earth after a spring rain. I turn toward her and lean in for a kiss. Our lips meet, spreading warmth through my chest, awakening my fire. Io presses her hips into mine. I groan against her lips. I slip a hand beneath her tunic to cup her breast. Io sighs, arching her back. We tear at each other’s clothing, desperate to remove any barrier between us. Her skin is heaven to touch, flawless and soft. She reaches down to my groin. My body responds instantly to her touch. I ease her onto her back. Her braid has come lose, hair as black as a starless night spills across the silky pillow.

“What?” She asks, raising an eyebrow.

“Your beauty has me spellbound,” I

breathe, as my eyes roam over the beautiful Goddess in my bed.

Io pulls me down for a kiss. The chaos of the last few days melts away. Her taste is intoxicating, like the first sweet summer strawberries. She trails her fingers down my back, leaving tendrils of fire in their wake. We move in perfect synchrony, loving each other back to life. I would conquer kingdoms for this woman. Level armies to reach her. No force in all of the realms could keep me from my Io.

"Let's marry," I say.

"But I don't have a proper gown," Io protests.

I laugh and Io pinches me. "I want to look perfect for you," she pouts.

"I'd marry you stark naked in front of everyone. I just can't go another minute without making you my wife."

Io's eyes brim with sparkling tears. "Alright."

I leave Io to dress. I pass an excitable Terra in the corridor. Io immediately dispatched a hand maid to bring Terra the news of our last minute wedding plans. Terra and the hand maid are engaged in frenzied wedding plans. Terra shoots me a wink as they pass.

"She looks stunning in green. But perhaps we should consider crimson?" The hand maid says.

"Crimson is divine. Yes, let's see what the dress makers can prepare on such short notice."

"You'll be surprised, my Lady. Elodie has worked miracles on shorter notice."

"Marvelous. I'll see to her makeup and hair. Please extend my thanks to Elodie. See to it that she has all that she needs."

"At once, my Lady," the hand maid says with a deep bow.

Terra smiles warmly, returning the bow. I smile at the exchange as I continue down to the King's Chambers. I nod to the Kingsguard at the double doors. I knock and wait.

"Come in," the King's voice booms from beyond the doors.

I enter the King's sitting room, closing the door softly behind me.

"Ah, Rowan! What can I do for you, my boy?" He says from behind a great oak desk before a great stained glass window.

"Your Grace, I have come to ask for your blessing to marry your granddaughter," I say taking a knee and bowing my head before my King.

"Sir Rowan McGlaughlin, Lord Commander of the Kingsguard, you bring an old man great joy. You have my blessing, son," the King says warmly.

I am surprised when the King pulls me to my feet and embraces me with love. I am over come with emotion.

"Thank you, Your Grace," I say.

True to his word, the King summons his event planners and staff. Over the next two weeks the Black Keep is a buzz with excited wedding preparations. Xavier finds me at Terra's insistence, tasked with preparing me for the exchanging of wedding vows. The royal seamstress must be a gifted enchantress to have prepared such a fine groom ensemble so quickly. I examine the intricate needlework on the breast of the tunic, swirling azure blue flames against a cream fabric stitched with golden thread.

"Don't forget to smile when Io walks down the aisle. Maybe cry a little?"

"I'll see what I can do," I say rolling my eyes. "I honestly don't know why the whole court needs to come. I have never spoken a word to the majority of them."

"It's just a show for the stuffy old ninnies. Just focus on your Bride," Xavier says.

"I'll only have eyes for her."

20

IO

"How did she make THIS with barely a moment's notice?" I ask in wonder. "It is exquisite..."

I gaze at the ravishing gown, running my fingers over the gossamer fabric. It looks like a burning fire, layers of over lapping delicate orange, yellow, gold, and red with a shimmering sheen are laid over a deep black, rippling skirt. The fitted black leather bodice is fashioned of black, iridescent scales. Sheer red sleeves extend down to the wrist. Terra deftly braids my hair into an elaborate style. She decorates the many braids with golden rings and fresh red, yellow, and orange wildflowers. When Terra turns me around to face the mirror, I do not recognize the woman staring back at me. I swallow a lump in my throat.

"I wish my Mother was here," I admit, cross at myself for saying it out loud.

"She is here, Io. She would not miss this day," Terra says, giving my shoulders a gentle squeeze.

I blink away tears as I nod at my friend smiling at me in the mirror. I start to feel dizzy as the time to go downstairs draws near.

"It's normal to be nervous," Terra assures me. "Just breathe."

Terra and my hand maid, Violet carry Ella and Finn down the stairs. I feel as though I am in a dream. I follow silently, fussing with my skirt. When we come to the doors of the Great Hall, my heart is hammering in my chest. I clutch at the door frame to steady myself. Music starts to play. It sounds muffled and far away. Terra takes my elbow and I jump.

"Rowan is waiting for you, Love. You'll be alright when you see him."

I give Terra and Ella a hug. Violet gives me a hug and I give Finn a kiss. I step through the threshold. I spot an unexpected face in the crowd, Hekate's ageless countenance beams at me. My breath catches and I flash her a disbelieving smile. I blink and she is gone. I shake my head and take another step. I turn my face forward. There he is, waiting at the end of the long red carpet, *Rowan.* He smiles when I meet his gaze. Tears come unbidden and I do nothing to stop them. I smile through them as I walk to my Husband. *It was always you my soul was waiting for.* When I reach him, he extends his hand to me. I place my hand in his and he draws me into his arms.

The Priestess starts to speak but, I do not

hear a word she says. I take in Rowan, dressed in a fine cream tunic embroidered with blue and gold flames over dark blue pants. He smells divine, eucalyptus and mint. His hair is braided in a similar style to mine, pulled away from his face to bring attention to his fine jaw and close cropped red-gold beard. His eyes look bright green today. When Rowan starts to speak, I come out of my daze.

"Io, I love you with all my soul. You are the mother of our beautiful son, Finn. I am yours in all lifetimes. Being your Husband will be the honor of my life. I will protect you and our children. I will love you with every breath I take."

"Rowan," I start shakily. "You are the missing piece of my puzzle. I cannot imagine the world without you at my side. Together we will build a beautiful life. Our family is my whole world. You are the greatest blessing that has ever been bestowed upon me. I am honored to be your Wife. I will love you for all eternity."

"May the Gods and Goddesses bless this sacred union! Rowan, you may now kiss your Bride," the Priestess says.

Rowan places a gentle hand on my cheek as we lean in for our first kiss as Husband and Wife. The great hall erupts with applause and spirited cheers. I feel uneasy being the center of so much attention. Rowan's calming presence helps to keep me from bolting out of the hall. I breathe in his familiar smell as I melt under his tender touch. My knees threaten to buckle but, he holds me steady in his arms. When we break away, Rowan whispers in my ear.

"I love you, my Wife."

"I love you, my Husband," I whisper back.

Rowan's smile makes my heart skip a beat. *I want to remember him, just like this. Strong, handsome, and gazing at me with pure love on our wedding day.* Violet carries Finn over and Rowan takes him from her arms. Violet embraces me and gives me a kiss on the cheek. Terra and Xavier descend on us. A crying Terra hands Ella to Xavier before pulling me into a tight hug. I rub her back and whisper to her.

"You're next!"

"From your lips to his ears," Terra jokes with a roll of her eyes.

We walk arm in arm over to our table. Rowan and Xavier walk beside us with our little ones. Grandfather stands as we approach the high table. He embraces us all in turn.

"My heart is filled with joy. Thank you for giving this old man a reason to celebrate."

"Thank you all for planning a grand last minute wedding," I say.

"Of course, dear heart," Rowan says, kissing the top of my head.

Selene kisses Rowan and Finn. She embraces me and holds me at arms length.

"You look beautiful, my love. Thank you for giving me a grandson. I am so happy to have you in my life."

"Thank you, Selene," I say giving her a

kiss on the cheek. "You raised an incredible son."

We take our seats and enjoy a spectacular circus show complete with hand balancers, aerialists, contortionists, and fire spinners. The aerialists are my favorite. I am enchanted by their every, graceful movement on the flowing silk fabrics. A woman dressed in a golden body suit climbs to the top of a red silk and inverts with ease. She hooks her knee over the fabric and wraps her body with the tail of the silk. She flashes a smile at her admiring crowd before cartwheeling through the air in a whirlwind of limbs and red silk. Rowan smiles at me when I turn to him. I give him a lingering kiss. He places his hand on my thigh beneath the table. I rest my head on his shoulder as we watch the golden acrobat take her bow. Ella seems particularly taken with the fire spinners, twirling flaming staffs and fire fans. Finn is delighted by a man who effortlessly balances a beautiful woman over his head as she bends her body into impossible shapes.

When the show has concluded the crowd erupts into riotous applause and cheers. The floor is cleared and the music swells as couples wander out for a dance. Rowan stands and offers me his hand.

"May I have this dance, Mrs. McGlaughlin?"

"You may," I say taking his hand.

Selene offers to hold Finn while we indulge in a dance. Rowan and I step onto the floor arm in arm. Terra gives me a wink as she and Xavier sweep by. She looks stunning in a spring green gown patterned with soft pink roses. Xavier flashes us a winning smile as he twirls Terra across the floor. Rowan places his right hand at my waist and holds my right hand with his left. He leads the way and I glide with him as my fiery skirts swirl around me.

"You are radiant, my bride," Rowan whispers in my ear.

"You are rather dashing, my groom," I whisper back.

The dance floor is a blur of colors and flushed, happy faces. The strum of lutes and the sweet timbre of violins echoes throughout the great hall. Bards fill the air with lively lyrics. Laughter and happy chatter can be heard from guests enjoying the feast at long tables positioned around the dance floor. I spot an older man seated alone, clutching a mug of mead. He has tan skin with deep brown eyes, salt and pepper hair, high cheek bones, and a square jaw covered with a close cropped graying beard. He is dressed in a simple dark blue tunic, black trousers, and leather boots. As our eyes meet he raises his mug to me and smiles. I feel a strange flicker of recognition.

"What's wrong?" Rowan asks, jolting me out of my thoughts.

"That man in the dark blue, sitting alone at the table. Do you know him?"

Rowan follows my gaze. "No, I have never seen him before."

"Neither have I...but, he seems familiar."

"Why don't you go check on Finn? I'll see what I can find out about this stranger."

"Thank you," I say, reaching up for a kiss.

Rowan leans down to kiss me gently. He walks me back to our table. Selene carefully passes a sleeping Finn to me. Rowan gives Finn and I a kiss before melting back into the crowd to investigate the stranger. Selene is swept away by Felix, the cook. Terra and Xavier are still dancing. I spot my Grandfather a few tables over laughing with King Roland who bounces a giggling Ella on his knee. I smile at the sight. I am so glad he accepted our invitation.

"It is truly a joyous occasion," a male voice says to my left, startling me.

I turn to see the man in the dark blue tunic standing a few paces away. "My apologies, Your Grace. I did not mean to startle you."

"It's quite alright. I don't believe we've met," I say eyeing him warily.

"I was a friend of your mother. I wanted to offer my deepest sympathies. I was devastated to learn of her passing," he says gruffly, his eyes mirroring my own pain.

"Thank you. May I ask how you knew her?"

"She was my wife," he says meeting my gaze.

My breath catches in my chest as his words slam into me. "You're my father?" I ask, aghast at his casual confession.

"Yes, Io. I am Seth, your father," he says steadily, gauging my reaction.

I feel hot and my head is exploding with questions I never hoped would be answered. Rowan and Grandfather suddenly emerge from the crowd. Grandfather looks murderous, staring at my father as though he wants to throttle him. Rowan looks to me. I give him a small nod to let him know I am alright. My father bows to Grandfather as he approaches.

"Your Majesty, you are looking well. Lord Commander, congratulations on your marriage. I wish you both a lifetime of love and happiness," my Father says.

"You always thought you could talk your way out of anything," Grandfather scoffs. "How kind of you to grace us with your presence after 20 years of abandonment."

"I mean no harm. I only wanted to pay my respects to Brigid and meet Io," my father says, holding up his hands in surrender.

"The respectful thing would have been not to set foot in Caelen after you abandoned my daughter and grand daughter to a life of servitude in Elaria."

"I will take my leave," my father says bowing to Grandfather.

"Good night, Io. Take care of that handsome boy," my father says, smiling down at Finn and I.

"Please, I have so many questions. Will you stay as our guest?"

I feel like that lonely little girl again,

watching fathers at the market carrying their giggling little girls. My mother loved me well. I had a happy childhood. I just always felt a deep ache over the absence of my father. I always wondered why I was denied one.

"I am sure we can find a spare room for the night," Rowan offers, giving Grandfather a pointed look.

"You will be responsible for him," Grandfather says to Rowan. "See that he is gone before sundown tomorrow."

"Understood, Your Grace," Rowan says with a bow.

"Good night, dear heart," Grandfather says. "I love you. Time for me to turn in for the night."

"Good night, Grandfather. I love you. Sleep well," I say giving him a kiss on the cheek.

Grandfather's Kingsguard materialize out of the crowd and escort him upstairs. The revelry continues, couples waltz across the dance floor in time to the music. Clusters of red faced men slosh cups of ale as their voices boom over the music. Giggling ladies of the court whisper the latest gossip as they cast furtive glances at the subjects. I long for the quiet of our chambers.

"Ready to retire for the night?" Rowan asks.

"You've read my mind," I sigh with relief.

"Seth, I'll show you to a spare room along the way."

"Thank you, Rowan. It was a long road. A feather bed would be a welcome sight."

I part ways with Rowan and my father in the corridor at one of the guest quarters. I carry Finn up another flight of stairs to the royal wing. The guards at the top of the stairs bid us good night. I thank them and wish them the same. I am relieved to kick off my shoes when I close the door to our chambers. I settle Finn in his bassinet. I fall back into bed and breathe a contended sigh. I close my eyes and replay our dream wedding. I see Rowan standing at the altar smiling at me. I feel warmth spread through my chest as I drift off.

The sound of the door jerks me awake. I prop myself up on my elbows to see Rowan slowly closing the door behind him. He walks over and sits beside me on the bed.

"Hello," he says, kissing me out of my sleepy daze.

"Hello," I murmur against his lips.

Rowan runs his fingers down my back, sending a shiver down my spine. He carefully unlaces the back of my dress. I stand and let the silky fabric slip from my shoulders, it pools on the floor like liquid fire. I smile as Rowan drinks in my naked form. He pulls his tunic over his head. My eyes roam over his chiseled chest and abdomen. I close the distance between us, running my hands down his chest. I undo his belt, slipping his trousers down. He kicks off his boots and trousers. He draws me into his arms, claiming my mouth with a fiery kiss that leaves me breathless.

I step back toward the bed. We intertwine,

exploring, kissing, and tasting each other. The feel of his bare skin on mine unfurls tendrils of warmth in my belly. I feel safe in his arms, I am home.

"I love you," he whispers against my throat as he trails kisses down my chest.

"I love you," I breathe as my eyes close and pleasure consumes me.

21

ROWAN

I watch the steady rise and fall of Io's chest as early morning sunlight lightens the sky outside our window. I memorize every curve of her face, the sweep of her dark lashes, the high bones of her cheeks, and her soft pink lips. *My wife.* I press a kiss to her forehead before I ease out of bed. I take a peak at Finn sleeping soundly curled next to Io's chest. I kiss his forehead.

I clean my teeth, dress quietly, and leave a note for Io on the bedside table. I head down to the guest quarters that Seth stayed in for the night. He answers after one knock, fully dressed and alert.

"Good Morning," he says.

"Good Morning. I was just heading down to the kitchen in search of some breakfast. Care to join me?"

"Lead the way."

We walk in silence for a time. Seth seems ill at ease in the Black Keep. *Painful memories, perhaps.*

"Thank you. For standing up for me," he says suddenly.

"I believe Io deserves an explanation after all these years. I was hoping that you could reconnect after all this time."

"It is not a pretty story but, she deserves the truth. I was unfaithful to Brigid and she left me. I did not even know that she was with child."

"We all have chapters we wish we could rewrite."

"You are kind to say so. I tried to make up

for my mistake. I stayed close but, out of Brigid's life as she asked. When I saw her with a baby, it broke my heart. I destroyed my family before my child even drew her first breath. I found work as a huntsman in the village outside of Castle Greenwood. I supplied the butcher with venison, turkey, rabbit, and pheasant. Brigid and Io would come to the butcher weekly to purchase meat for the castle kitchens. I watched my girl grow up from afar. I made sure she was fed. It was my way of loving and caring for her."

"You should speak with her. She wants to know you. Losing Brigid unexpectedly has been hard for her. You two can make up for lost time."

"You are a good man, Rowan. I am grateful that you and Io found each other. Thank you for caring for my daughter and grandson."

"They are my whole world. We would like you to stick around."

Seth and I grab some warm bread, scrambled eggs, and bacon from the kitchens. We carry our breakfast back up to the chamber I share with Io and Finn. I know Io will be up and about by now. She answers the door dressed and looking lovely as ever. She smiles warmly at the pair of us.

"Good morning, I hope you slept well," she says to her father.

"I did. Thank you for your generous hospitality. We brought up some breakfast."

"I'm needed down in the training yard. Why don't you two catch up over breakfast? I'll be back by lunch," I say giving Io a quick kiss.

"Thank you," she whispers in my ear.

I smile at my beautiful wife and give Seth a nod before heading out. I find the Master at Arms barking at several flustered squires when I enter the armory. They scurry into the training yard carrying armfuls of shields and wooden practice swords.

"Don't be too hard on the lads, Gerald. They were probably up to the wee hours trying to woo the kitchen maids after the wedding celebrations."

"Perhaps I have forgotten what it was like to be young," Gerald sighs.

"You don't look a day over thirty to me."

"That's the wedded bliss talking," Gerald chuckles. "Let's get to it so you can get back to your lovely wife."

Several knights look slightly green from their evening drinking spree and late night shenanigans. Gerald pretends not to notice, drilling them hard. One gangly fellow vomits all over his squire. I send two squires to fetch water buckets to rinse off the poor lad. Xavier appears as the gagging squires are dousing their mortified friend.

"Yikes. Gerald's pushing them hard today. Some of these knights look like they did not sleep a wink. Some clearly cannot handle their ale."

"It has been a rough morning indeed. How are Terra and Ella?"

"Lady Lita arrived this morning. Terra is eager to hear her thoughts on Ella's gift."

"I hope she can help Ella harness her magick."

"I think she is in good hands. How is Io getting on with her long lost father?"

"I left them over breakfast. I hope they have a good talk. I think he genuinely cares for her."

"I hope so. Io deserves healing after all this time."

Xavier and I jump into the sparing line, testing each knight to his limit. It feels good to work my muscles and go through the motions. The ring of steel sharpens my focus as my feet follow the familiar foot work. I slashe my blade through the air. I am drenched in sweat when Sir Gerald calls the break for lunch. Xavier offers me a drink from a water skin.

"Care to join us for lunch?"

"I'll get cleaned up and head down with the family."

My legs ache as I walk back up to our chambers. I enter to find Io and Seth playing with a smiling Finn. Seth offers him a stuffed bear that Terra made for him. They turn as I close the door softly behind me.

"How was training?" Io asks.

"Let's just say Sir Gerald showed no mercy for the knights who may have indulged a bit too much in last night's revelry."

"That sounds like Gerald," Seth chuckles. "I'm heading down to visit Brigid's grave. I'll see you both at dinner."

"Give her my love," Io says, standing to embrace her father.

Seth gives Io a kiss on the cheek. "I will, dear heart."

Io has drawn me a bath which I gratefully sink into. She offers me a wash cloth and a bar of soap. Finn squeals with delight when she dunks him into the tub next to me. I give him a kiss as Io gently washes his back.

"Xavier invited us for lunch. He said Lady Lita arrived this morning to meet Ella."

"I hope she does not foresee anything grim in her future," Io says.

"We'll hope for the best. Xavier says Terra trusts her. Terra loves Ella as though she were her own flesh and blood. She would not trust Ella with just anyone."

"That is true. Let's go see for ourselves."

Io bundles Finn up in wooly grey socks, warm brown cotton pants and shirt, and a navy sweater my mother knitted for him. I dress and pull on my boots. We make our way down to Terra and Xavier's cottage on the sea cliffs. Terra greets us at the door and invites us in. Xavier is serving up bowls of chicken soup and buttered bread. Lady Lita is holding Ella on her lap. Little Ella can't take her eyes off of Lady Lita. They seem to be exchanging thoughts that the rest of us can't hear. Lady Lita greets us when we enter the cozy kitchen.

"Hello, newlyweds. And who is this handsome little man?" She says, smiling at a curious Finn as he peers at her unfamiliar face.

"Lovely to see you again Lita. This is Finn," Io says giving Lita a one armed hug.

"Thank you for coming all this way to meet with Terra," I say.

"Thank you for having me," Lady Lita says graciously. "Ella is a remarkable child. It has been my pleasure."

Io and Finn take a seat opposite Lady Lita and Ella. I notice Terra seems a bit anxious, wandering about the kitchen tidying things. Io watches Terra and glances at me with concern.

"Can I help you with anything, Terra?" Io offers.

"Oh no, I am fine. Sorry, just straightening up," Terra says with a forced smile.

Io gives her a look but, does not pry. Terra comes to sit beside Lady Lita. Ella reaches for her and Terra takes Ella into her arms. I look to Xavier who has a similar look of distress.

"So what is the plan for Ella's training?" I ask, cutting right to the heart of the matter.

"I feel that Ella would benefit from some

time among other young mages," Lady Lita says gently.

Terra seems on the verge of tears. Xavier rubs her back as he places a steaming mug of tea in front of her.

"She is too young. She has already lost her birth parents. I will not send her away," Terra says firmly.

"Ella is no ordinary child. She will need guidance to control her psychic and telekinetic abilities. I believe that being among children like her will help ease the burden."

"I can guide her! We will keep her safe. She needs us. Mara left her in our care," Terra argues.

"Terra, I know you love her deeply. Believe me when I say that I do not suggest this lightly. Ella is different. She can be a danger to herself and others without proper training. Her power will only grow. Psychic abilities can drive one to madness. I will oversee her training personally. I do not seek to rob you of your child. You can be by her side every step of the way," Lady Lita says gently taking Terra's hand.

"I'll come with you," Xavier says, placing his arm around Terra's shoulders.

Terra looks up to him with tears shining in her icy blue eyes. The tension in her shoulders melts as she nods. Ella reaches up to touch Terra's face. Terra nods and presses a kiss to the top of her head.

"Take time to gather your things. We will leave when you are ready," Lady Lita says.

Io gives Terra a sad smile with a nod of encouragement. My heart goes out to them both. They will miss each other terribly. Lady Lita rises from her chair and suddenly collapses to the ground.

"Lita!" Terra gasps.

I crouch by her side. Her eyes have rolled back in her head and her body convulses. I turn her onto her side. Xavier places a seat cushion under her head.

"What is happening?" Io asks.

"A vision," Terra murmurs.

Lita stills suddenly and lets out a pained gasp. Xavier pours a cup of water. Lita blinks and slowly tries to sit up. I help her into a sitting position. Xavier offers her the cup of water. Lita accepts it with a trembling hand.

"Are you alright, Lita?" Io asks.

"What did you see?" Terra asks in an apprehensive tone.

Lita takes a small sip of water. She raises her eyes to meet Terra's worried gaze.

"Ella. I saw Ella as a woman grown, standing in a tower…" Lady Lita says in a daze. "I sensed a dark presence."

"Darkness in Ella?" Terra asks.

"No, a dark presence trying to force her hand. Someone will try to control Ella's power, use it for great evil," Lady Lita says, her eyes unfocused and wide with horror. "She is in great danger."

"Did you see this person?" Io asks.

"A tall figure in a scarlet cloak, a pale slender hand with a golden serpent ring clutching a bright ruby in it's fangs."

"A face would be more helpful but, that is a start," Xavier says in an attempt to lighten the mood.

Io and Terra glare daggers at him while I stifle a snicker. Ella looks to Lady Lita. Lita gazes into Ella's deep blue eyes. She nods and smiles.

"Ella says she will save us all," Lady Lita says. "Of course you will, my darling."

Terra hugs Ella to her chest. Xavier helps Lita back into her chair. Io places her forehead against Terra's, whispering softly as she rubs her back. Xavier passes out bowls of chicken soup and plates of fruit. The tension gradually subsides as we all dig in. Terra's spirits slowly lift and I see that fierce determination in her eyes once more. Io smiles at me across the table. I nudge the toe of her boot with mine, returning her smile. Io spreads a quilt on the floor for Finn and Ella. Terra deposits a few wooden toys that Xavier made onto the quilt, a little horse, a rattle, and a bird. Ella offers the wooden horse to Finn who squeals with delight.

"He will miss her," Io says sadly.

"We'll visit often," I promise.

"We must. Or else we will need to give him brothers and sisters," Io says with a sidelong glance.

"That can be arranged," I say, pulling her close to my side and kissing her cheek.

22

IO

Terra seems to be her usual self after a delicious lunch and afternoon tea. Xavier has her laughing again. *Thank the Goddess for this man. He will take excellent care of Terra and Ella.* Rowan and I take our leave. A cold wind blows in from the stormy sea. I watch the waves crash against the massive boulders along the rocky shore below. A flicker of movement catches the corner of my eye, I turn to see a white hawk soaring by. He turns his head in my direction, we lock eyes for a second before he dives down below the edge of the sea cliffs in pursuit of prey I cannot see.

"Did you see that hawk?" I ask Rowan as he adjusts a sleeping Finn in his arms.

"I have never seen a pure white one before," he says. "Handsome fellow."

"Indeed," I say, as we wind our way along the path back to the castle gardens.

We find Felix in the kitchens going over dinner plans with his cooks. The smell of roast makes my stomach growl. Huge pots of potatoes boil away on the stove top. Kitchen maids chop fresh rosemary and sage for the creamy herb butter. Another group is preparing a dark leafy green salad with chunks of roasted pumpkin, cranberries, and walnuts. The pastry chef is decorating a delectable spice cake with cream cheese frosting and fresh flowers from the garden. Rowan stops to talk with Felix while I pluck two apples for us from a heaping basket. I cannot wait for dinner.

When we get back to our chambers,

Rowan gently lays Finn in his bassinet. I offer Rowan a shiny red apple. We kick off our boots and enjoy our apples on the couch by the fire. I snuggle next to Rowan as the fire warms my cold feet. We set aside our apple cores for the compost pile. I lean my head against Rowan's shoulder, my eyelids slide closed. I slip into a dream.

I am walking up a stone spiral staircase. I can hear muffled voices above me. I look up to see an eerie green light high above me illuminating my way. I continue to ascend. The voices growing ever clearer.

"This is what you were born to do. I will give you everything your heart desires, Ella. Give me your arm. Do not fret, child. I only need a few drops. You are the key," a female voice echoes down from the tower room above.

"You gave me your word that no one would come to harm!" Ella shouts. "I can never face my family again after what you've done. Now I am alone!"

"Women like us do not have families or

friends," the woman says flatly. "We are meant for a greater purpose. It is a lonely road. Love is weakness, Ella. You have been given a gift. I will not see it go to waste."

I run as I hear the women struggling and glass crashing to the stone floor. Ella screams in frustration. The sound of a vicious blow connecting increases my pace. I force air in and out of my lungs as I gain the landing. When I burst through an ancient wooden door, Ella is sprawled unconscious on the floor. A woman in a scarlet cloak hovers over her still form.

"BACK AWAY FROM HER!"

The woman turns. I stare into her pale narrow face and dark green eyes. Her lips curve up in a condescending sneer as she slowly rises to her feet, clutching a wicked, gleaming dagger dripping with Ella's blood.

"Ah Io, presume. I am honored to meet the Dragon Queen in the flesh. Allow me to introduce myself, I am Farrah Steele of Moorsend."

"I've never been," I say sweetly. "To what do we owe this pleasurable visit?"

"I have searched far and wide for a girl of Ella's talent. The magick in her blood is just what I need to complete my life's work."

"Do tell," I say, circling Farrah in an attempt to get close to Ella.

"I can't very well spill all my secrets. We have only just met," Farrah says with an admonishing look.

"I can tell we will be fast friends. Perhaps we can discuss it over tea?"

Farrah throws her head back and laughs. A hearty cackle that stokes the fire of my simmering rage.

"You are quite the charmer, Your Grace. I do applaud your effort to keep a cool head. But we're done here."

Farrah turns on her heel and strides toward a large pewter cauldron suspended above a roaring fire in an enormous hearth. She raises her dagger, giving the hilt a firm tap with her slender finger. Three crimson drops fall into the simmering pale gold liquid. The blood turns the pale gold to a vibrant orange hue. I shield my nose against the noxious fumes as my eyes burn. The fire flares, bringing the mysterious orange potion to a rolling boil. Farrah inhales deeply, closing her eyes.

"That's it," she murmurs faintly.

I silently creep over to Ella's side. I am relieved to find that true to her word, Farrah only made a shallow slice on the inside of Ella's forearm. It looks as though Farrah bludgeoned her with the vase that is shattered on the ground beside her. I gather Ella into my arms. I glance up to see that Farrah is completely ignoring us. Ella's eyes flutter open. I firmly clamp my hand over her mouth. Her body goes rigid and she tries to pry my hand loose. She blinks and relaxes when she recognizes me. I hold my pointer finger to my mouth. Ella nods. I help her to her feet and we slowly back away toward the exit, keeping our eyes trained on Farrah's back. She is reading from a large, ancient tome. I do not recognize the tongue she is speaking. The flames rise and the sound of rushing of wind fills my ears. Ella and I creep through the door way. When we reach the stairs, we run for our lives.

I wake with a jerk, alarming Rowan who was sleeping soundly beside me. He leaps to his feet, hand gripping his sword hilt. He blinks the sleep out of his eyes as he surveys the room, breathing a sigh of relief when he sees no danger is present.

"Bad dream?" He asks.

"Yes-s, s-sorry," I say shakily. "I don't think Lady Lita told us everything she saw in her vision."

Rowan pours water in the kettle. He hangs it over the fire and comes back to sit beside me as I recount my dream. He does not interrupt as I recite every last detail I can remember. His brow furrows in deep thought."

"Moorsend..." Rowan says, standing up.

He strides over to the bookshelves. He returns to the couch with a large dusty volume. He lays it on the table. I lean forward to peer at the pages as he starts skimming through the book. He stops at a large map that spans across the yellowed pages.

"Ah!" He says pointing in triumph.

Scrawled in loopy script above Rowan's finger is the name '*Moorsend.*'

Rowan withdraws his hand so I can examine the whole map. I scan the landscape and find Caelen in the south. Moorsend is at the northernmost tip of Veridian. A journey to Caelen from Moorsend would take weeks.

"I have never heard of this place," I say puzzled. "This map looks centuries old. I do not think that Moorsend is on any of our present day maps."

"It is not," Rowan says. "I remember learning about it. It was once a flourishing kingdom known for its devotion to magickal study and powerful Mages. But their last ruling Queen became power hungry. She killed her sister for the throne and sought to conquer her neighboring kingdoms with dark magick. The kingdoms of Veridian united to rise up and crush her. Legend says that Moorsend is nothing but an old ruin now."

"Maybe some old bloodlines survived," I say, tracing my finger along the map.

My thoughts keep turning to Moorsend as I dress Finn for dinner. I run a brush through my hair. Farrah's face haunts me as I pull a dress from my wardrobe. *Where are you now?*

Grandfather rises from his seat when we arrive at the table. Finn and I give him a hug. Selene and my father are seated next to each other, talking like old friends. Terra and Xavier appear with Ella. Lady Lita walks alongside them, her ravishing beauty turns the heads of several kingsguard. Grandfather welcomes her. I take note of the way their eyes linger on each other. *Curious.* Mother told me that Grandmother died when she was only 12 years old. Grandfather never remarried. There is an ease between the two of them. Even though Lady Lita does not look a day over 40, I know she is much older. Possibly hundreds of years. *Agelessness, perks of being a Mage, I suppose.* Grandfather is strong and still looks handsome at 60 years. I would not begrudge them the companionship.

"I have been meaning to speak with you, dear heart," Grandfather says turning to me.

"Of course," I say, snapping out of my wandering thoughts.

"The time has come for me to step down. You will succeed me as Queen of Caelen."

"What?" I say, completely taken aback. "Are you unwell, Grandfather?"

"No, my dear. Do not fear. I am in good health but, I am an old man now. It is time for me to pass the crown to my successor. Caelen is ready for a new ruler. I believe that you are more than up to the task. You will be a fine Queen."

"I don't know anything about ruling a kingdom," I say, fighting the rising panic in my chest.

"You will not be alone. I will be here to guide you. You will have royal advisors of your choosing. Rowan will be at your side as your King."

"How long do I have to decide?"

"I hoped we could announce your Coronation on the morrow."

My hands are slick with sweat and my corset suddenly feels too tight. Rowan leans over to ask if I am alright. I barely hear him over the pounding of my heart.

"Very well," I say, praying my quavering voice does not betray me.

"I know this is a lot to place on your shoulders. I was terrified when I ascended the throne. It is natural to fear the unknown. A good ruler does not thirst for power and a life of luxury. A good ruler understands that her people and the prosperity of the kingdom are her responsibility. A good Queen must be brave, clever, strong, and selfless. I can think of no one better to lead us. You are the Blood of the Dragon. With you on the throne, Fire will Reign."

23

IO

The last two months have been a blur of meetings with foreign dignitaries, lessons on the history of Veridian, learning the crests of the high houses, grueling hours in the training yard with Terra, and tedious seamstress measurements for my coronation dress. I have only seen Rowan when I fall into bed at night. I keep Finn by my side throughout the day. He does not like the parade of strangers. Terra brings Ella along with her to keep Finn company. Grandfather convinced Lady Lita to live at the Black

Keep so that Terra does not have to move to her mountain stronghold. I have chosen Grandfather and Terra as my royal advisors. Xavier will be succeeding Rowan as the Lord Commander of the Queensguard.

"Again," Terra says.

I huff as I take my stance, raising my sword once more. Terra attacks. I have become familiar with her habits. When she steps to her left, I spin away and slash at her vulnerable right side. The wooden practice sword cracks her in the ribs. She flinches away for the briefest moment and I seize the opportunity to kick her legs out from under her. Terra crashes to the ground with a grunt. I place my sword at her throat.

"Bravo," Terra groans. "You have earned your freedom."

"Finally," I exhale, wincing at my own aches.

I extend my hand to help Terra to her feet. We come out to the practice yard everyday just before dawn. The knights don't start until after breakfast. The first streaks of sunlight are reaching above the mountain peaks. We extinguish the torches we used in the horse trough. Terra returns our practice swords to the armory. We make our way to the great hall for breakfast. Rowan and Xavier are waiting for us with the babies. Finn has started eating soft foods. Rowan has some mashed pumpkin for him this morning. I give my loves good morning kisses before easing myself into a chair. My every muscle screaming in protest. Rowan takes my hand. I feel his healing magick spreading through me like warm soothing balm.

"Thank you," I breathe.

He offers Terra the same healing remedy which she gratefully accepts. Xavier and Ella shower Terra with good morning kisses.

"You two have a nice time beating each other senseless?" Xavier asks.

"It was a rough morning," I admit.

"Io is becoming quite the formidable opponent," Terra says with a grin.

"Terra would not have it any other way," I say with a laugh.

I add a spoonful of honey to my lemon ginger tea. The first sip feels like heaven. The walk to the great hall in the early morning crisp fall air has chilled me to the bone. Rowan passes me a plate of scrambled eggs and pancakes. Finn reaches for me with pumpkin covered fingers. I pull him into my lap. He plucks a fluffy piece of egg from my plate. We share my breakfast.

Ella has been practicing using a fork and spoon. She is much cleaner than Finn at the end of breakfast. I mop up my little pumpkin boy before we leave the table. I am dreaming of a nice hot bath before I head off to the library for more studying. Terra heads home with Ella to clean up.

"I'll meet you two in the library," she says, giving Finn a kiss before she departs.

Ella waves good bye. Finn returns her little wave. Rowan gives us a hug and kiss before heading to the training yard with Xavier. Back in our chambers I force myself out of the bath. The hot water feels amazing on this cold fall morning and I wish I could linger. I give Finn some milk before I get dressed. I select a golden gown with a high neckline and long flowing sleeves. The front of the bodice has buttons, for easy access when Finn wants to nurse again throughout the day. The skirt is pattered with delicately embroidered roses. I like the way it catches the morning sunlight streaming through the library's floor to ceiling windows. A fire is burning merrily in the massive hearth. This room is one of my favorites. Finn and I settle down on the couch in front of the hearth. I brought some of his toys and a warm blanket to spread on the rug. Terra and Ella join us.

"I did not want to leave my warm bath," Terra whines.

"Neither did I. Probably the hardest thing I will have to do today," I joke.

"What's on the agenda?"

"Picking up where I left off yesterday, *The*

History of Veridian," I say, placing the heavy book on my lap.

"Quite the page turner," Terra says. "It is perfect for lulling you into a midmorning nap."

"I'll do my best to resist."

I pull my parchment and quills out of my bag. Taking notes helps me absorb this vast sea of knowledge. Terra settles Ella on the floor with Finn. I told her about my dream. She has been pouring over every book in the library in search of information about Moorsend. Today she has a stack of ancient scrolls and a tower of weathered books. The library doors open and we turn to see Lady Lita enter.

"Good morning, ladies," she says in greeting.

"Good morning, Lita," Terra says.

"Come to see Ella?" I ask.

"I have. I also was looking for a warm place to spend the morning," she admits.

"Please join us," I say, gesturing to the couch.

Lita plays with the children while Terra and I struggle to keep our eyes open. These books are not exactly thrilling pieces of literature. I keep having to reread passages when I come back to after nodding off. Terra and I take turns waking each other. Finn and Ella think this is hilarious. I smile at their squeals and giggles.

"I think you two need a break," Lita says, taking pity on us. "Shall we take the children for a walk in the garden?"

"Marvelous idea," Terra says, not bothering to stifle her yawn.

"I could use some fresh air," I say, rising to my feet.

We all bundle up before making our way to the garden. Ella just started walking. Finn, a few months younger, is eager to catch up with her. Ella toddles through the rows of vegetables. Finn crawls after her. He pulls himself up on a wooden bench and reaches for me. I hold his hands in mine, he takes a few steps with my help. A broad smile spreads across his face, his bright green eyes sparkle. This boy has stolen my heart. *Just like his father.*

Ella chases after a fluttering blue butterfly. Terra jogs after her. Lady Lita hangs back.

"Terra tells me that you had a dream about Ella."

"Yes, I did. I was climbing a staircase in a stone tower. There was an eerie green light illuminating my path. I could hear Ella and a mysterious woman arguing at the top of the tower. They fought. When I got to the top, the woman was taking some of Terra's blood for a spell. She introduced herself as Farrah Steele of Moorsend."

"I have not heard mention of Moorsend in centuries," Lita says. "House Steele was one of its noble houses. I believe they were royal advisors."

"Have you ever been to Moorsend?"

"Long ago, I attended the coronation of Queen Gisele Caraway. She was the last ruler of Moorsend. Her sister's hunger for power brought the kingdom to ruin."

"Do you believe that there were survivors?"

"It is possible. Many folk fled Moorsend in search of a fresh start when the Queen descended into madness. The Queen and all her forces were put to death after their defeat. Moorsend was burned to the ground."

"Why would Farrah be so obsessed with finding Ella?"

"Farrah was once a great Sorceress. She studied under the finest Mages. She excelled in her training and was one of the Queen's favorites. She became obsessed with an old prophecy about the *Mage's Blood Moon.* The prophecy foretells of a Blood Moon that occurs every 500 years. A mage who performs a blood rite under the Mage's Blood Moon will be granted infinite power. Power over the elements, the ability to walk between worlds, immortality, and even the power to summon the dead from beyond the veil. The mage will need the blood of 1,000 magickal souls. The spell is extremely difficult. It will draw on Farrah's life force, to fail will mean certain death."

"Those are high stakes. She must have a compelling reason to take such a risk."

"The reason we all go to such lengths, love. Farrah lost her beloved, Sir Adam Blackburn, in the Queen's war. She was destroyed by the loss. She spent every waking moment searching for a way to bring him back."

"How can we stop her?"

"I believe it is Ella's destiny to stop Farrah."

"We will stand with her. We must start preparing now."

"I am at your service, Your Grace. Ella will be ready."

24

IO

"Did you sleep at all last night?" Terra asks, brushing my face with powder.

"I tossed and turned for a while. Do I look that dreadful?"

"Not to worry. I'll fix you up," Terra assures me as I stifle a yawn.

"Do you think anyone will notice if I slip away after the coronation for a nap?"

"I'll cover for you," Terra says with a smile.

Terra helps me into the flowing red gown

that the seamstresses made for my coronation. The fabric is soft and silky against my bare skin. The neckline is trimmed with delicate gold lace. A burgundy leather corset layers over the top of the bodice. The sleeves flow down to my elbows. The voluminous skirt floats around me when I twirl. Violet places a gold chain at my throat with a glittering golden dragon pendant. She places ruby earrings on my ears. Terra brushes my hair out. Violet paints my lips and brushes gold dust on my eyelids.

"You are radiant, Your Grace," Violet says stepping back so I can look at myself in the mirror.

"I have you ladies to thank for that. I could never achieve this on my own."

"It's time," Terra says.

We make our way down to the great hall via a secret passage. Rowan and Xavier are waiting for us at the opposite end. Rowan stops talking mid sentence when he catches sight of me. He pulls me to his chest.

"You are beautiful, my Queen," he whispers in my ear.

"Thank you, my King," I whisper back.

Rowan and Xavier lead us into the great hall. Rowan takes my hand and escorts me to the throne where Grandfather is waiting. He looks wonderful, dressed in a dark blue tunic, black pants, and a wolfskin cloak draped over his shoulders. He embraces me and kisses my cheek. We turn to face the crowd.

"It gives my heart great joy to welcome you all to the Black Keep today for my Granddaughter's coronation. It has been my honor to be entrusted with the Kingdom of Caelen all these years. The time has come for me to pass the crown on to another."

Grandfather turns to me. "Io Aurelia Flynn-McGlaughlin, do you swear to treat your subjects with kindness, honor, and dignity?"

"I so swear."

"Will you defend the Kingdom of Caelen

from enemies and if necessary, lay down your life in the defense of your people?"

"I will."

"Do you swear to heed sound counsel from you advisors and weigh your decisions carefully?"

"I so swear."

"I, King Eamon Killian Flynn, crown you Io Aurelia Flynn-Mcglaughlin, Queen of Caelen, Blood of the Dragon, our Sovereign and Savior. Long may you reign!"

"LONG MAY SHE REIGN!" the gathered crowd bellows.

Grandfather removes the golden crown from his head and places it gently on mine. His eyes shimmer with tears and I feel my own eyes burn as he smiles at me. Grandfather bows deeply. The entire assembly in the great hall bows in unison. I can scarcely breathe as I take in the sight. A roar of applause and shouts erupts. Music swells and the floor is cleared so that the dancing can begin. Grandfather leads me to the throne.

My legs are shaking, I am relieved to sit. Rowan takes the seat on my right. Grandfather sits on my left. Terra hands Finn to Rowan before taking a seat between Grandfather and Xavier who holds Ella on his lap. My Queensguard surround the throne dais, keeping a watchful eye as members of the court approach to offer blessings and kind words. Servants bring platters of fruit, roast meat, chicken, warm bread, greens, roasted vegetables, and spiced cider.

Couples twirl on the dance floor as music fills the hall. The kitchen maids deliver platters of food to the tables. Servants fill cups with wine, ale, and spiced cider. I hope it will be socially acceptable to slip away soon. Being the center of attention makes me uneasy. Rowan pats my hand. I meet his eyes.

"We'll take our leave soon. Just let them down several goblets so we can slip away unnoticed."

"You know me all too well," I say with a smirk.

I scan the room. Snippets of idle chatter and peels of laughter can be heard between the strum of lutes. A flash of scarlet catches my eye in the far right corner of the hall. My blood turns to ice as I take in the unmistakable face of Farrah Steele. I place my hand on Rowan's arm. He follows my line of sight. He signals to the Queensguard nearest him. Rowan whispers in the guard's ear. He nods and slips into the crowd. I see four more guards follow him. I keep my eyes trained on Farrah. She makes pleasant conversation with the guests around her. When she catches sight of the guards, she melts into the crowd. I start to rise. Rowan catches my wrist.

"Don't take the bait."

"She'll escape," I hiss.

"She did not come here for Ella. She came to try to get to you. Don't walk into her trap."

"We can't let her get away."

"We will stop her, Io. No harm will come to Ella. This I promise you."

I sit back. My gut twisting at the thought

of this woman so close to my family. Terra looks over and raises her eyebrows. I mouth *Farrah,* nodding my head in the direction I last saw her. The color drains from Terra's face. She hugs Ella to her chest as she rises from her seat. She moves to my side.

"You saw her?" Terra asks in horror.

"Yes. Rowan sent the Queensguard after her."

"We should close the gates. Lock the Black Keep down until she is found."

"I don't think she came to make her move, only to show her face and strike fear in our hearts," I say.

"Stay in the castle tonight," Rowan says. "We'll prepare a room for all of you and post guards."

"Thank you," Terra says.

"We'll keep Ella safe. I promise," I say, giving her hand a gentle squeeze.

Terra gives my hand a squeeze. Grandfather has gone to mingle with his friends. Terra takes his seat and Xavier moves into Terra's seat.

"What's going on?" Xavier asks.

"Io saw Farrah in the crowd," Terra says with a shiver.

"What are we sitting here for?" Xavier asks.

"I sent some guards after her," Rowan says. "I don't like this. It feels like a trap to lure us in."

The guard Rowan dispatched approaches the table with his four companions. He offers Rowan a red envelope.

"We pursued her to the sea cliffs. She dropped this before transforming into a white hawk. She flew north towards the mountains," the guard reports.

"Thank you, Jon," Rowan says. "Make sure the men stay alert tonight."

"Yes, Your Grace."

Jon and his men return to their posts. Terra takes the red envelope from Rowan's hand. She examines the black wax seal, a hawk clutching a snake it its talons. Terra breaks the seal. She reads the short message in neat script. She holds it out for the rest of us to read.

Enjoy your brief reign, Dragon Queen. In 16 years time under the Mage's Blood Moon, the world will be mine and I will bring about your doom.

"You know people mean business when the threat rhymes," I say.

"I'll pluck her feathers and roast her alive," Terra says flatly.

"Kind of her to leave a card," I say. "No one writes any more."

"We won't let her ruin this night," Xavier says firmly.

"When she returns, we'll be ready," Rowan says. "Now hand over Ella and you two go dance."

I take Ella from Terra, giving her a fierce hug. "Everything will be alright," I whisper. "Now go dance with your love."

Terra gives me a teary smile. Xavier leads

her to the dance floor. I watch the tension melt as he twirls her around. The color returns to her cheeks, a smile pulls at her painted red lips. Her powder blue gown hugs her slender figure and brings out her bright blue eyes. She is a vision tonight. I see a few jealous ladies of the court looking down their noses at her. Terra does not notice, she only has eyes for Xavier. *We'll be dancing at their wedding soon.*

"You're a good friend to her," Rowan says.

"I am simply returning the love she gives me," I say. "You should tell Xavier to propose. He'll never find another woman who comes close to Terra."

"I'll get right on that," Rowan says with a chuckle.

My Father approaches our table, I stand and embrace him.

"Please sit with us."

"Thank you, dear heart. I am proud of you. You will be a fine Queen. I am sure your mother is smiling down on you."

"Thank you, Father. I am glad that you are here with us. I would like Finn to know his grandfather."

Finn reaches for my father who takes him with a smile. He bounces Finn on his knee and offers him a wooden horse from his coat pocket.

"Did you carve that yourself? Such exquisite detail."

"I whittle from time to time," he says modestly. "Ah, I made this one for you."

My Father pulls out a wooden dragon. I take it, examining the intricate scales, the curves of the tail, and the fine pointed teeth.

"It is beautiful. Thank you," I whisper, embracing my father.

"You are welcome, my love," he says, patting my back.

Terra and Xavier return from the dance floor, flushed and merry. They greet my father warmly. Terra takes Ella from Rowan. Finn offers Ella his little horse. My heart melts. Ella offers Finn her favorite bear. I want to freeze this moment in time so I can come back to it whenever I need to be with my favorite people. A sanctuary I can escape to whenever the world feels dark. Farrah is out there, bidding her time, plotting to take all that I hold dear. *I'll be here, ready to answer with fire and blood.*

ACKNOWLEDGMENTS

Thank you to my family and friends for supporting my writing. Your love and support mean the world to me. I'd like to thank designer Brizine from 99designs for this epic book cover. You truly brought my vision to life.

I have read many stories written by amazing authors that have touched my heart and soul. I hope that the stories I tell will warm hearts and inspire readers to write stories of their own. Becoming an author has always been a dream of mine. I am beyond grateful to be living my dream!

ABOUT THE AUTHOR

Amy Elizabeth Johnson was born and raised in Hawai'i. She is a wife, mother, Army Veteran, and Circus Artist. Epic fantasy, adventure stories are her all time favorite reads. When Amy is not writing you can find her in the sky on her aerial silks. Cooking while dancing to music in the kitchen is also a favorite pastime. Amy loves to travel with her Ohana, her all time favorite humans.

www.ingramcontent.com/pod-product-compliance
Lightning Source LLC
Chambersburg PA
CBHW020946310726
48980CB00001B/78

* 9 7 9 8 9 9 8 6 3 5 1 5 1 *